Marcus unexpectedly reached out and ran his thumb over her lower lip.

Her eyes locked with his, and a jolt of sexual awareness coursed through her, leaving her breathless and dizzy.

Marcus's eyes had darkened, and she could see a tiny muscle twitch near his jaw. Then he smiled and, without taking his eyes from her, snaked his arm along the padded back of the couch, letting it lie there, his fingers just touching her shoulder.

"Nice?" he said softly.

Jenna couldn't speak. That light touch scorched. She couldn't recall ever being so acutely aware of another human being. When his thigh brushed against hers, she bit down hard on her lip.

This is Marcus, she said to herself, dazed. She'd never felt like this about him—about anyone....

Dear Reader,

Celebrate the holidays with Silhouette Romance! We strive to deliver emotional, fast-paced stories that suit your every mood—each and every month. Why not give the gift of love this year by sending your best friends and family members one of our heartwarming books?

Sandra Paul's *The Makeover Takeover* is the latest page-turner in the popular HAVING THE BOSS'S BABY series. In Teresa Southwick's *If You Don't Know by Now,* the third in the DESTINY, TEXAS series, Maggie Benson is shocked when Jack Riley comes back into her life—and their child's!

I'm also excited to announce that this month marks the return of two cherished authors to Silhouette Romance. Gifted at weaving intensely dramatic stories, Laurey Bright once again thrills Romance readers with her VIRGIN BRIDES title, *Marrying Marcus.* Judith McWilliams's charming tale, *The Summer Proposal,* will delight her throngs of devoted fans and have us all yearning for more!

As a special treat, we have two fresh and original royalty-themed stories. In *The Marine & the Princess,* Cathie Linz pits a hardened military man against an impetuous princess. Nicole Burnham's *Going to the Castle* tells of a duty-bound prince who escapes his castle walls and ends up with a beautiful refugee-camp worker.

We promise to deliver more exciting new titles in the coming year. Make it your New Year's resolution to read them all!

Happy reading!

Mary-Theresa Hussey

Mary-Theresa Hussey
Senior Editor

Please address questions and book requests to:
Silhouette Reader Service
U.S.: 3010 Walden Ave., P.O. Box 1325, Buffalo, NY 14269
Canadian: P.O. Box 609, Fort Erie, Ont. L2A 5X3

Marrying Marcus

LAUREY BRIGHT

SILHOUETTE *Romance*

Published by Silhouette Books

America's Publisher of Contemporary Romance

SILHOUETTE BOOKS

ISBN 0-373-19558-3

MARRYING MARCUS

Copyright © 2001 by Daphne Claire de Jong

This edition published by arrangement with Harlequin Books S.A.

® and TM are trademarks of Harlequin Books S.A., used under license.
Trademarks indicated with ® are registered in the United States Patent
and Trademark Office, the Canadian Trade Marks Office and in other
countries.

Visit Silhouette at www.eHarlequin.com

Printed in U.S.A.

LAUREY BRIGHT

has held a number of different jobs, but has never wanted to be anything but a writer. She lives in New Zealand, where she creates the stories of contemporary people in love that have won her a following all over the world.

Chapter One

Anticipation sizzling in her blood, Jenna Harper scanned the passengers from the recently landed Los-Angeles-to-Auckland flight. Backpackers in jeans and boots, business people in tailored suits, parents with tired-eyed children, a middle-aged couple whose grandchildren swarmed to them as they appeared from the customs area.

Among those waiting at the arrivals gate, Pacific Islanders in flower-patterned prints, and an Indian woman's butterfly-wing sari, created splashes of early-morning color.

By Jenna's side her best friend, Katie Crossan, shifted impatiently from one foot to the other. Katie's sister, Jane, hitched her youngest into her arms while her husband restrained the older two, who were becoming restless.

"When's Uncle Dean coming?" the four-year-old demanded.

"Soon," his grandmother assured her.

The entire Crossan family had turned out to welcome Dean home. Even Marcus, his elder brother.

Jenna wondered if Marcus would have come if Katie hadn't begged him to drive her and Jenna to the airport at Mangere.

He stood a little aside from the rest of the tightly knit group, taller than any of them, including his father. Dark hair was ruthlessly combed back from his angular, intelligent face; his hands were thrust into the pockets of gray-green trousers, which he wore with a cream shirt.

He turned his head a fraction and caught Jenna looking at him. One black brow lifted slightly, and then a corner of his long, firm mouth. His storm-cloud eyes were disconcertingly penetrating.

Jenna gave him a nervous smile, flicked a strand of fine, light-brown hair from her cheek to behind her ear and looked away, searching the next wave of arrivals.

Marcus was older than Katie and Dean, the twins who were born when he was nearly six and Jane five.

Katie and Jenna had agreed that although they'd miss Dean like crazy, the scholarship that had taken him away for four years to America would give him the chance to move out of Marcus's formidable shadow. But the waiting had been hard.

Marcus saw him first. "Here he comes."

Katie broke away from the group, shrieking Dean's name before her arms circled his neck and he caught her, swinging her off her feet.

The children, suddenly shy of this stranger, hung

about Jane, impeding her and her husband as they too pressed forward.

Jenna couldn't help a smile of pure joy, bubbles of it bursting inside her like champagne, but she made herself wait. As soon as the family greetings were over, Dean would look for her. And she enjoyed just drinking in the sight of him.

He was not as tall as his brother, but his hair was nearly as dark and had a nice wave. His features were regular and his eyes a warm blue. Film-star looks. And when he saw his family, his face showed unashamed affection that to Jenna's eyes made him even more handsome.

Mr. Crossan gave him a quick hug, Mrs. Crossan wiped a tear after hugging him in her turn, the three children clustered around Jane as she kissed her younger brother's cheek, and her husband clapped him on the shoulder.

Jenna took a step forward, then halted when the tall, tanned blonde behind Dean, whom she had assumed was another passenger patiently waiting for the family to move out of the way, went to his side. Unbelievably he turned to put an arm about her.

It was like a slow-motion movie. Jenna's mouth dried, her blood froze. She was almost suffocating, standing immovable as a puzzled hush settled on the group just yards away.

Dean smiled down at the girl and said happily to his family, "This is Callie—we're getting married."

Chapter Two

The world stopped for Jenna, although all about her people were moving, calling out to others, hugging and kissing, helping to push carts piled high with luggage.

The family came to life. Katie squealed, punched Dean's chest. "You didn't tell us!" His mother gave Dean another hug, embraced the girl and kissed her cheek. His father shook her hand, then Dean's.

Dean hadn't even looked at Jenna.

Everything around her faded and turned gray, and the jumble of sounds became muffled. She was numb.

A hard hand closed about her arm, so tight that it hurt. And she was glad, because she needed something to persuade her she could still feel. Marcus's deep voice next to her ear said, "Do you want me to get you out of here?"

Yes, she thought, but said thinly, when her woolly tongue found itself, "No." He couldn't abandon his family. "Of course not. You…h-haven't said hello to your brother."

She dragged her eyes from Dean and saw that Marcus was looking extremely grim, his gaze on his brother's face not welcoming at all. He returned his attention to her. "Neither have you. Are you up to it?"

Overwhelming embarrassment and panic gripped her. Maybe she was going to be sick. Afraid to open her mouth again, she tried to nod.

"You look as though you're about to fall over," Marcus said bluntly.

Jenna gritted her teeth, forcing out words. "I won't." She held her breath, hoping to bring some color into her cheeks.

The group around Dean was surging toward her and Marcus. He didn't let go of her arm as Dean saw them and bounded over, abandoning the baggage cart.

Jenna molded her lips into something approximating a smile and instructed herself to breathe again. Marcus had moved ahead of her, his free hand outstretched so that Dean had to stop and take it, giving Jenna a little more time.

Marcus said unemotionally, "Hi, Dean. Congratulations. And welcome home."

"Thanks." Dean's other hand gripped his arm. "You haven't changed a bit, Marc."

Behind him, Katie shot Jenna an anxious look. Then Dean turned to Jenna and held his arms wide, eclipsing his sister. "Hi, Jen! Sweet of you to turn out at this time of the morning. How are you?"

He hugged her, not seeming to notice that her own

arms hung lifelessly at her sides. "You have to meet Callie," he said.

She supposed she did.

Stepping back, she almost collided with Marcus, her shoulder touching his chest, but he didn't move. And neither did she, buttressed by the solid feel of him right behind her.

She turned the hurting smile to the girl's face. "How nice to meet you."

"You too." Callie had a warm American accent, a genuine smile. "I've heard a lot about you."

What? her mind asked frantically. What did Dean say about me? Did he tell you I've been stupidly in love with him since we were children? That I thought he would come back and marry me? That next to Katie and his mother I thought I was the person he was closest to in all the world?

"Katie's best friend," Callie said, "and room-mate—except here you call it a flatmate." She screwed up her nose and laughed. "Isn't that right?"

"Yes." Jenna couldn't say any more. She wanted to scream, cry—run. Pride kept her upright, smiling.

Callie looked at Marcus. "And you're Marcus," she said. "The big brother." She gave him a frank, open look, her eyes wide and candid, and the smile turned from friendly to appreciative. "He's told me all about his family."

"And yet he hasn't told us a thing about you," Marcus said.

Callie laughed again. "He wanted to surprise you."

"You are certainly a surprise." Marcus paused. "A welcome one, of course. I hope you'll enjoy New Zealand."

"I'm looking forward to it, and to getting to know you all. Oh—and Jenna too."

The afterthought was kindly meant, Jenna knew, but it made her conscious that she wasn't really family, she didn't belong.

Jane's children had commandeered the baggage cart, and one of the bags slipped. While Callie helped to reorganize the luggage, Jenna blindly turned away, following an instinct to flee.

Marcus was in her way. His fingers circled her arm again for a second. "Just stay here." His voice held a note of command.

She stood there while he exchanged a few quick words with his parents and Katie, who threw her friend another worried glance.

Then Marcus was back at her side, his hand on her elbow. "Come on."

She didn't ask where they were going, so relieved that he was taking her away from this nightmare that she didn't care. "Katie…?" she said feebly as he whisked her across the polished floor.

"There's room for her in Mum and Dad's car, and she won't want to be separated from Dean. That's something Callie will have to get used to—how close the twins are."

And of course with Callie sharing the back seat, there'd be no room for Jenna.

Dean's parents expected him to stay at their home, just half an hour out of Auckland, until he'd settled. They hadn't been expecting him to bring a fiancée, but there'd be no problem putting up an extra person in the big house where they'd brought up their family—the house Jenna had known almost as well as she knew the much smaller home she'd shared with her mother next door.

In the parking area the cool air chilled her, although the gray morning sky was turning to blue, with high white clouds drifting across it.

Marcus guided her to his sleek maroon car and opened the door for her. He didn't speak again until they were on their way out of the airport complex, driving between green fields gradually being overtaken by new buildings.

Then he said, "I told the family I'd join them later. Have you had breakfast?"

"Breakfast?" Jenna repeated vaguely.

"Something to eat. What most people have in the morning."

"No." She and Katie had been too rushed and too excited to eat breakfast at that early hour. She didn't see what relevance it had.

"Neither have I," Marcus said. "We'll stop on the way."

Jenna didn't argue, although she had never felt less hungry. Like his younger siblings, she'd developed a habit of listening to Marcus.

When they reached the outskirts of the city he found a restaurant and ordered juice, toast and pancakes for two, and made Jenna drink hot, strong coffee. With sugar.

"That's better," he said, after she had eaten two slices of toast and pushed the empty coffee cup away. "You're beginning to look human again."

"I'm never at my best in the morning," she said.

Marcus gave her a thoughtful look. "I'm sorry, Jenna."

She gazed down at the white ceramic salt cellar on the table—shiny and smooth. "Thanks," she said, "for breakfast." *And for rescuing me. Stopping me from making a complete fool of myself.* "I'll pay my share."

"Don't be silly." A lean hand caught hers as she made to open her purse. "I'm paying." He removed his warm, strong fingers from hers and took out his wallet.

In the car she said, "Maybe I should just go home."

Katie had taken it for granted that Jenna would spend the weekend with the Crossans. It was lucky, she'd said, that her twin had chosen to fly in on a Saturday. They needn't take time off from work.

Jenna had thought it lucky too. Now she wished she could plead pressure of work, an emergency, any excuse not to be there.

His hand on the ignition key, Marcus turned a searching look on her.

"An engagement is a family affair," Jenna suggested, her voice strained. "And I'm not family."

Gently he said, "It smacks a bit of sour grapes, you know. Do you want to make us all feel guilty?"

"No! We—you've all been looking forward so much to having Dean home again. I want everyone to be happy for him and...and Callie."

"Very noble." His tone was extremely dry. "I suspect you'd like to slap him silly, really. I know I would. I felt like thumping him at the airport."

Jenna blinked up at him, surprised that Marcus should feel so strongly on her behalf. "I don't suppose I'd be missed," she said.

He made a small, scornful noise in his throat. "You know better than that. Of course you'd be missed." He paused. "If it's what you want, I'll take you back to the flat and tell the family you're not well." But he sounded reluctant.

They'd guess that the only thing she was nursing was a broken heart...wouldn't they? And if Katie did believe in a sudden sickness, concern about Jenna being ill and alone would spoil her delight in her brother's return.

She chewed her lower lip, undecided. "I suppose your whole family is sorry for me."

"Katie might be. I guess you've told her how you feel?"

After a moment Jenna shook her head. "Not really. I mean...not in so many words." She'd assumed that Katie knew—but then she'd assumed Dean felt the same. And she'd been totally, unbelievably wrong. "I thought everyone knew." She lifted her eyes to his almost accusingly. "You did."

His mouth moved in a slight smile. "I don't think my parents have recognized yet that you and the twins are actually grown up. They've never taken your adoration of Dean seriously. And Jane has been pretty much occupied with her own family for the past few years. I take it you haven't been exchanging love letters with my little brother?"

She'd always signed her regular letters with "Love, Jenna." And Dean had sent his love in return when he wrote, but his much-less-frequent letters were addressed to both Jenna and his twin, and when he phoned the flat, whichever of the girls answered the phone called out to the other, and they'd eagerly swapped the receiver between them and passed messages until Dean had to hang up.

Jenna had never minded sharing. She'd been grateful that Katie didn't either. Twins, even nonidentical ones, enjoyed a special bond. She understood that. Did Callie? She said, "Not love letters, exactly."

She and Dean had known each other so long there was no need to express their feelings in extravagant words. They would have felt silly doing it.

"Dean isn't cruel," Marcus said consideringly. "But he's not always terribly bright about people's feelings. Probably he just never noticed. The consequence of growing up together. He didn't see what was right under his nose practically all his life."

If Marcus was right, staying away today would only fuel any suspicion that might enter anyone's head—including Dean's. Or Callie's. Somehow that would be worse than anything.

His voice became brisk. "How are your acting skills? You used to be pretty good as a kid. Especially if it was a question of saving young Dean's bacon."

But Marcus, she recalled, had always seen through her subterfuges on Dean's behalf. As he'd seen through her today and stepped in to avert what might have been a dampener on the family reunion, an embarrassment to everyone.

When she remained silent, he added, "It's entirely your choice, but if you come along I promise I'll make it as bearable as I can—and we'll leave early."

Jenna took a deep breath. "I'll come."

She couldn't read the look he gave her. His mouth was very firm, his eyes dark and probing. Then he put out a hand to squeeze hers before starting the car.

* * *

It was just as bad as she had imagined.

Marcus parked in the asphalt area in front of the sprawling old house with its gabled windows, the walls and decorative trims freshly painted in honor of Dean's return. Brushing past scented lavender and frilled pinks in pots at the side of the steps, they went in the big front door that was expectantly open and through the wide hallway.

The adults were sitting around in the family room with cups of tea and coffee, while the children darted between the chairs and chased one another in and out of the French windows opening onto the tree-fringed lawn and the fenced pool.

Marcus explained their delayed arrival by saying he'd needed something to eat after being dragged out of bed at some ungodly hour at his younger sister's insistence and then stuck at the airport for nearly an hour.

"You could have eaten here," his mother chided.

"I was too hungry to wait." He smiled at her. "And going without breakfast didn't do Jenna any good, either."

Mrs. Crossan gave her a sympathetic look. "You are a wee bit pale." She dropped her voice and murmured anxiously, "You're not upset about Dean's engagement, are you, dear?"

"I think it's wonderful," Jenna lied valiantly. "Callie's beautiful, isn't she? And Dean looks so happy."

"Well, yes." Mrs. Crossan's eyes turned to the couple, and Jenna saw the smile she couldn't help. "They are very happy."

Dean and Callie had freshened up, and Callie

looked even more gorgeous than she had at the airport. Dean hardly took his eyes off her for long enough to wave to his brother and throw a careless "Hi, again!" at Jenna.

She should be glad he didn't look at her too closely, but instead she felt a jealousy so strong and painful she had to bunch a fist at her midriff to stop it hurting so much.

Marcus's fingers closed over hers and pried them apart. "Is there coffee on?" he asked no one in particular. "Let's get some, Jenna." He hauled her with him into the big, sun-filled kitchen.

"We just had coffee," she said as he dropped her hand and went to the machine in a corner of the counter.

"Have some more. Or can I get you something stronger?"

Jenna shook her head. She needed her wits about her. "No."

He pulled two mugs from hooks under the cupboards and filled them, stirring some sugar into hers. "Here."

Katie came in, a pile of cups and saucers in her hands. "Are you all right, Jen?"

Trying not to sound too hearty, Jenna injected a faint note of surprise into her reply. "I'm fine. Are you pleased to have your brother home? Don't answer that. Silly question."

Katie grinned, obviously unable to suppress it. "I never realized how much I missed him." The grin fading abruptly, she added, placing the cups on the counter, "Callie's a bit of a bolt from the blue, though.'' Her eyes worried, she asked, ''He...he hadn't said anything about her to you, had he?''

''Not a thing.'' Jenna made her voice cheerful. ''If he'd told anyone it would have been you.''

Marcus interjected, ''A whirlwind romance? If even you didn't know anything, Katie...''

''He did mention her a couple of times, but I never twigged she was anyone special, and he hadn't said anything about her recently. He says he was scared she'd turn him down, and he didn't want to come home and have us all know he was nursing a broken heart. She only agreed to come to New Zealand with him a couple of weeks ago, and he decided to keep it secret until they got here, so he could see our faces when he gave us the news.''

Thank heaven he hadn't seen hers, Jenna thought. She curled her hand around her hot coffee mug, ignoring the discomfort.

Katie added thoughtfully, ''And I have a suspicion he was afraid she might change her mind before he got her on the plane.''

Jenna forced a smile. ''Well, it's a nice surprise, isn't it?''

Dubiously, Katie agreed, ''I suppose so. Are you sure you're okay with it, Jen?''

Hoping she looked bewildered and innocent, Jenna said, ''Of course. Dean's very happy. And I'm happy for him. Aren't you?''

Hesitantly, Katie said, ''I thought it would be you and him. Even when we were kids you said you were going to marry each other.''

Jenna's laugh should have earned her an Oscar.

"We were—what?—eight years old? Come *on*, Katie!"

"Sometimes when we were older it kind of looked like you were more than friends."

Jenna had thought so. They'd exchanged kisses from time to time. She'd imagined that, like her, Dean was keeping their relationship on the level of a warm, intimate friendship while they both worked hard at their degrees and were too young and impecunious for marriage.

After they'd graduated, the scholarship had come up for him to study in America. He'd asked Jenna's opinion, stressing how long he'd be away from home, and she'd somehow concealed her panic and dismay and said of course he must take it, a chance like that wasn't to be missed.

The kiss he gave her then was definitely not a brotherly one, and she'd seen it as a promise, a pledge, an unspoken commitment to a shared, if deferred, future.

She'd held on to that memory for four years. And now she wondered if Dean even remembered it. Certainly it had held none of the significance for him that it had for her.

Painfully putting her newfound insight into words, Jenna said, "We grew out of it. If there'd been anything serious, Dean wouldn't have left me to go to the other side of the world for years. Would he?"

Marcus added, "Wishful thinking, Katie. Very nice for you, to match your twin and your best friend, but in real life our childhood sweethearts grow up and marry other people."

"Did yours?" Katie asked, temporarily diverted.

"Of course," Marcus answered. "And I didn't lose a moment's sleep over it."

Katie switched her attention back to Jenna. "Have I been daydreaming?"

"I won't lose a moment's sleep," Jenna echoed Marcus, trying to sound as convincing.

Either Marcus had sown the seed of doubt, or Katie decided to take her cue from Jenna's denial. "Well, that's a relief," she said. For a long second her eyes rested thoughtfully on her friend, before she began stacking cups and saucers in the dishwasher.

Jenna and Marcus finished their coffee, and all three of them rejoined the others. Neighbors dropped in to say hello, and a cousin phoned inquiring after the traveler. Dean invited her and her parents and boyfriend to come over.

A party atmosphere developed. Some of the guests sat out on the tiled patio, and children were allowed to jump in the swimming pool in its fenced enclosure at the back of the house. Jenna talked and laughed and even conducted a conversation with Callie and Dean, finding that Callie was exactly what she looked like, a golden California girl. She'd been studying at the same university as Dean, although they had met only a few months ago.

"And when he opened his mouth and I heard that cute accent," Callie confessed, her hand caressing Dean's arm, "it was love at first sound."

"She thought I was Australian," Dean teased, grinning adoringly at her. "I had to educate her about the difference between Kiwis and Aussies."

"It took him all night." Callie swept him a flirtatious look.

"Slow learner." Dean shook his head, returning the look.

Jenna's smile felt set in concrete. She didn't think the two of them would have noticed if everyone else in the room had disappeared in a puff of smoke.

Marcus laid a hand lightly on Jenna's shoulder. "Dad says you haven't seen his latest acquisition," he said. "He wants me to show it to you."

Gratefully she followed Marcus to the back lawn, where a shade house was tucked into a corner screened by pink-flowered manuka shrubs. Mr. Crossan was a keen amateur orchid grower, and when Marcus ushered her into the shade house, they were surrounded by pots and hanging baskets of the exotic, distinctive flowers.

The air was cool here, and the bark chips that covered the ground muffled their footsteps. A damp rich smell pervaded the glassed-in area.

Jenna walked along the narrow space between the tiered benches holding rows of orchids, many of them smothered in blossom. Delicate, spidery varieties and large opulent ones were ranged along both sides, the flowers spilling over their pots, some almost to the ground. "Which one are we looking at?"

"The pink one over here." He guided her to it with a hand lightly on her waist and stood behind her as she studied the pale, frilled blooms, flushed with gold at the throat.

Tentatively she touched a fingertip to a delicate petal. "It's very pretty."

"It's called Puppy Love," Marcus told her, slanting her a rather dry sideways glance. "Personally I prefer the more sophisticated varieties."

Staring down at the plant, Jenna blinked away tears. Puppy Love. A fragile flower. And though orchids lasted longer than other flowers, there came a time when they too withered away and died.

She turned away from it, and Marcus moved to let her pass him, returning along the row. "We needn't hurry back." He strolled after her, hands in his pockets. "No one will miss us for a while."

No one would miss Jenna. Self-pity threatened to overwhelm her. But they'd miss Marcus for sure. Marcus was a dominant figure in any gathering, not only because of his height. There was a quiet air of confidence and authority about him that even his family acknowledged.

Maybe it came from being the eldest. Jane was nearly his own age, but having two much younger, mischievous siblings might have given him an exaggerated sense of responsibility.

She halted before a plant exploding with extravagant bronze blooms. They blurred before her eyes, and she bit down fiercely on her lower lip, squeezing her eyes shut, taking a long, deep breath.

Marcus said, "One of Dad's prizewinners. Magnificent, isn't it?"

"Yes." Her voice was husky, but his casual tone steadied her. "What...what's it called, do you know?"

"The name should be on a marker in the pot." Marcus leaned across to part some spiky leaves, and his sleeve brushed her arm. "Dark Delight."

As he drew back he slanted her a swift glance, and his hand briefly rested on the skin of her arm, a comforting caress. His breath stirring her hair, he said, "It will get better, you know. Hard to believe right now, maybe, but I promise you it's true.''

She gripped the edge of the bench in front of her. ''I don't want your sympathy, Marcus.'' It would be too easy to turn and let him take her in his strong arms and hold her while she wept out her bewilderment and heartache. She had to get through this day without cracking, in order to keep her pride, at least, intact.

''Sorry.'' As far as the space would allow, he moved away from her.

''I didn't mean to seem ungrateful.''

''I'm not looking for gratitude, Jenna.''

''You've been awfully kind.'' She blinked the tears away and managed to face him.

A strange expression crossed his hard features, almost as if he shared her pain. He lifted a hand, and his thumb wiped an escaped salty droplet from her cheek. ''It will soon be over.'' His thumb strayed to her abused lower lip, where she had bitten into it. Unexpectedly he dipped his head and pressed his firm mouth gently to hers.

Chapter Three

It lasted only a second, but a faint warmth seeped into her cold heart, and when he stepped back, saying, "Can you stand to go back inside?" she nodded, feeling somehow stronger, braced for the fray.

Jenna helped Katie and her mother rustle up an impromptu meal. Some visitors had drifted away, but there was quite a crowd around the big table in the spacious dining room, and Jenna's lack of conversation went unnoticed. Marcus took a seat next to her, shielding her from Callie and Dean on his other side.

After the dishes were disposed of, Marcus found Jenna hanging up a tea towel in the kitchen, carefully straightening the edges. "Anytime you want," he said, "we can go."

Thankfully she took the hint. Steeling herself, she parried Katie's suspicious surprise that she'd decided to go home after all, using the excuse that this was a family occasion, and repeated her congratulations to Dean and Callie.

Within minutes she was releasing a sigh of relief as she fastened her safety belt.

Marcus started the car and edged out of the driveway. "You can let go now, if you want," he said.

Cry, she supposed he meant.

Although she'd been fighting tears for hours, now the urge to weep had left her altogether. She sat dry-eyed and silent beside Marcus all the way back to the city. The sunlight dancing on the water of the west harbor as they sped alongside it seemed to mock her bleak mood of despair.

Leaving the high speed zone, Marcus glanced at her as he eased off the accelerator. "Will you be all right on your own?"

"I won't slit my wrists," she promised.

He smiled. "I know you wouldn't. If you'd rather come to my place, I have a spare room."

She shook her head. "Thanks, but no. You've been great, Marcus."

"It doesn't cost me anything, and much as I'd like to wring his neck, I couldn't allow Dean's homecoming to turn into a disaster."

He might have been sorry for her, but his main concern was his family. Because she was close to his brother and sister, Jenna too had always come under his protection, but she guessed that if she threatened their happiness he'd sacrifice her without a second thought.

Which was right and natural. Only it didn't make her feel any better.

Marcus said, "It's a pity your mother's so far away."

For the past three years Jenna's mother had been

living in Invercargill, at the other end of the country, with her second husband. "I'm too old to run to my mother," Jenna said.

She'd learned early in life that running to her mother didn't solve anything. Karen Harper loved her daughter, but at times her own problems had been too overwhelming for her to cope with Jenna's, as well.

Marcus cast her a glance. "If you do need someone to run to," he offered, "I'll be around."

She managed a pale smile. "Thanks, but I don't think so."

"Independent little cuss, aren't you?"

"I've always tried to be."

"Had to be, I suppose. It must have been tough, losing your father so early."

"I never really knew him—I only have a few hazy memories. It was hard on my mother, though. I'm glad she's found someone else."

"We promised to keep an eye on you, you know, when she went to live down south."

Jenna had been just short of twenty then, still at university and living in a students' hall. "I don't think she meant me to be a lifelong burden on your family."

He turned the car into the quiet suburban street where she and Katie lived. "You're not a burden, Jenna. You're a friend. And that's going to make things difficult for you over the next few months, perhaps. You won't confide in Katie, will you?"

She wasn't sure if it was a question or a disguised warning. "No." It was going to be difficult enough for Katie, adjusting to a stranger having a claim on her twin. Knowing that her closest friend carried a torch for him would add extra stress.

"Here you are." The car stopped outside the building. "I'll come in with you."

"You don't need to—"

He ignored that, and it was just as well. When she opened the door of the flat they were greeted by disaster. Water was dripping from the ceiling and running down the walls, spreading a huge dark stain across the carpet.

"Hell!" Marcus surveyed the mess. "It's either a burst pipe or someone's left a tap running in the flat above you."

It was hours before it was all sorted. The upstairs owners—away for the weekend—were tracked down, a key located, the forgotten tap turned off. And then came the cleanup.

Marcus stayed despite Jenna's protest. He made phone calls, shifted furniture, helped her mop up water, and tracked down a carpet-cleaning firm who sent a couple of men who moved more furniture and set huge electric fans about the place to dry out the carpets they'd lifted and folded back.

Over the roar of the motors Marcus said, "Well, that settles it. You'll have to come to my place after all."

"I don't know if—"

"You can't stay here," he said. "Is all you need in this bag?" He lifted the tote that she'd previously put essentials into, assuming that she would stay the night at the Crossans'.

"I'll just change my clothes," she said, capitulating. Her cotton trousers and shirt were wet and grubby. "I won't be long."

One thing about the past few hours, she'd scarcely had a chance to think about Dean and his bride-to-be.

Marcus's apartment was a direct contrast to the cheery muddle Jenna and Katie lived in. The main room was large and airy, the sofas long and luxurious and precisely aligned about a solid rimu coffee table that held one elegantly formed pottery dish. Theirs was invariably cluttered with magazines, paperback books left open and facedown, junk mail, the TV remote control, probably an opened snack food bag and quite likely a hair dryer and bottles of nail polish.

Marcus's books and magazines were arrayed on shelves, probably in alphabetical order, Jenna thought, and there wasn't a sign of clutter.

The spare room he ushered Jenna into was equally sparse and neat. "The bed's made up." He placed her bag on the end of it. "Make yourself comfortable. I'll give Katie a ring to let her know you're here and break the bad news about your flat."

She unzipped the bag, shook out the skirt and top she'd packed, and hung them in the empty wardrobe to get the creases out.

Shutting the door, she caught her reflection in the mirror on the outside. Her face looked lifeless, her mouth pale and tremulous. Rummaging in the bag, she brought out a lipstick and swept a little color over her lips, then rubbed at her cheekbones with her knuckles. At least she could make an effort not to look like a Victorian maiden about to go into a decline.

In the living room, Marcus was replacing the receiver on the phone. "I'll have a shower and get out of these clothes." He still looked remarkably well groomed, despite the wet patches and dirty splashes on his shirt and trousers. "Are you hungry?"

She hadn't thought about eating. Marcus was probably starved. "I could cook something while you're in the shower, if you have anything…"

"I'll take you up on that. Raid the freezer. Use whatever you want."

Forty-five minutes later they sat down in the dining area to honey-glazed chicken with rice and peas. "This looks great," Marcus told her. "And it deserves a good wine to go with it."

He poured a New Zealand Chardonnay for them both and smiled at her as he sipped at it, but he didn't offer a toast.

Apparently having a broken heart hadn't destroyed Jenna's appetite after all. She ate everything on her plate and finished the wine in her glass.

Marcus refilled it. They didn't talk much, and when he pushed away his plate she said, "I didn't make a dessert, but you have cheese in the fridge."

"I'll get it and put coffee on." He cleared their plates and returned with a couple of cheeses and some crackers on a ceramic square. "Coffee coming up. Do you want more wine?"

"Why not? I'm not going anywhere."

Marcus filled her glass again, and she lifted it to her lips. She could feel the alcohol-induced flush on her cheeks.

Slicing himself a piece of cheese, Marcus shot her

a quizzical look. "It's not the end of the world, you know."

Unaccountably irritated, she said resentfully, "I don't need you to tell me that!"

"Okay." He held up a hand in a gesture of truce. "Take some time to wallow in your misery. But remember there's a life out there waiting for you."

And she'd already wasted four years of it. "You're right," she said, and raised her glass. There was no point in dwelling on what might have been. "Here's to the future," she said resolutely.

Marcus matched her gesture, giving her a look of approval.

Jenna drained her glass. "Is there more of this?"

He hesitated, poured some for her, then emptied the remains into his own glass.

By the time they left the table, the world looked a whole lot better. Marcus vetoed her feeble effort to deal with the dishes, and when she yawned, he said, "You've had a long day. Bedtime, I think."

"Yes." She blinked at him, not moving, and yawned again.

Marcus gave a low laugh and stood up, grasping her hands to haul her to her feet. The room tilted, and when he released her hands she clutched at his arms to steady herself. "Ooh! Too much wine."

"Very possibly," he agreed, and slid an arm about her waist to guide her. "Come on."

In the spare room he led her to the bed, switched on the bedside lamp and stripped back the covers for her. "Can you manage now?" he asked, straightening. "You know where the bathroom is."

"Yes. Thank you, Marcus."

"You might not be thanking me in the morning." He surveyed her with critical amusement and a hint of tenderness. "Good night, Jenna."

He bent and brushed his lips over hers—a fleeting kiss of friendly comfort, but enough to upset Jenna's already precarious balance, and as he lifted his head she swayed, so that instinctively he put his arm about her waist again to steady her.

She leaned against him, thankful for the solid feel of him, and her hands slid around his shoulders. She raised her face, found his mouth with hers and kissed him with fervor, her eyes closed, fiercely shutting out all thought. She didn't want to think, only to feel something other than grief and humiliation.

And Marcus, perhaps understanding her need, returned her kiss beautifully, satisfyingly. He put his other arm about her and brought her closer, making her feel warm and wanted. Like a desirable woman.

But then he drew back, and his hands left her waist to curl about her arms and hold her away. Although his eyes glittered disturbingly and there was a flush on his angular cheekbones, his voice was steady. "Enough. Get some sleep, Jenna. I'll see you in the morning." Then he walked to the door and shut it firmly behind him.

Jenna slept surprisingly well but woke with a leaden feeling in her chest and a slight headache.

A hangover, she supposed. All that wine last night...

She closed her eyes again. That only brought the memory more vividly to her mind, and she groaned. She and Marcus, of all people, locked in a passionate kiss. What had possessed her? And now she was going to have to face him. She could hear him moving about already, the bathroom door closing, his footsteps in the passageway.

No use cowering in bed, he would probably come and rout her out of it, anyway. Reluctantly she threw back the covers and got up.

By the time she'd showered and dressed, the aroma of frying bacon was wafting through the dining area. Trying to look casual and unembarrassed, she went to the kitchen where Marcus was standing at the stove, breaking eggs into a pan. "That smells good."

He turned and smiled at her. "Good morning. I heard the shower and figured you'd soon be ready for breakfast."

"Can I help?"

"Make toast if you like. The bread's over there."

It wasn't until they'd finished eating and she'd had her second cup of coffee that she gathered the courage to say, "About last night...I'm sorry."

"What for?"

"For being so...stupid. I'd had too much to drink or I wouldn't have..."

"Kissed me?" His lips curved. "I wondered if you'd remember. You needn't apologize, Jenna. It may have escaped your notice, but I enjoyed it." He paused. "I thought you did too." His eyes held a question.

Heat burned her cheeks. "I would never normally have—I didn't mean to—"

"No need to explain." He stood up abruptly. "Want to help me get these dishes out of the way?"

Later he took her back to her flat.

"I'll try to get it looking a bit less like a disaster area before Katie arrives home," she said. "It will give me something to do."

"She won't be here for a while. I told her there was no point while the carpet's still drying."

"That's okay. I can do with some time alone."

He gave her a sharp look but didn't argue. "Let me know if you need anything," he said. "I'll be home. And if your place is still in a mess, you and Katie can both sleep at mine tonight."

After he'd left her she picked her way around, flattened some of the carpet that had dried, moved the machines to where they'd do the most good, and cleared paths through piled furniture to beds and the kitchen.

Remembering the orderliness of Marcus's apartment, she was spurred into an orgy of tidying and cleaning. So when Katie arrived she was on her knees, head and hands deep in a kitchen cupboard while she wiped down the shelf from which she'd removed all the pots and pans.

It wasn't until she emerged and sat back on her heels, wiping a strand of hair from her eyes, that she realized Katie wasn't alone.

Dean grinned down at her. "What are you doing?"

"What do you think I'm doing?" she asked crossly. Yesterday she'd dressed carefully, if casually, and put on makeup, and he'd hardly glanced at her. *Now* she was a total mess and he was looking her over as if he'd never seen her before. "Where's Callie?" she asked him.

"Jet lag caught up with her and she couldn't stay

awake. Marcus said you'd had a flood here, so I thought you girls might need some help.''

He didn't look jet-lagged. He looked wide-awake and heartbreakingly handsome, and she wished he were anywhere but here. ''There isn't much we can do,'' she said, ''until the cleaning firm has been in again and fixed the carpets back in place, once they're dry.''

''You look busy.''

''I just had this urge…I'll be finished here in a few minutes.''

She hoped they'd go away, but instead the two of them stood about the kitchen talking, and helpfully handed her things to put back in the cupboard.

Afterward they all sat drinking coffee, and it was almost like old times until Dean pushed back his chair, saying, ''I'd better get back. Callie should have woken by now.'' Apparently he couldn't bear to think of her spending any waking moment without him.

When he'd left, Katie gave Jenna a searching look. ''Are you really okay?''

''Tired, after spending half the night getting rid of the flood, but otherwise I'm fine.'' Without pausing for breath, Jenna asked, ''How did you get on with Callie?''

''You can't help liking her…''

''That's good,'' Jenna said enthusiastically. ''It's important that you two get along. Not that Dean would have picked a girl you wouldn't like.''

Katie hesitated, then refrained from pursuing the subject. ''I'm sorry you got stuck with the cleanup here. I would have caught the first bus back, but Marcus said there was nothing I could do that the two of you hadn't done already.''

''He was right, there was no need for it. Marcus was great.''

''He's good in a crisis, our big brother. And I suppose he thinks of you as another little sister.''

''I suppose,'' Jenna agreed, but the memory of last night's kiss surfaced with sudden clarity, and unexpectedly she felt her cheeks flush.

Katie noticed. Her eyes widened. ''Jenna...? You and Marcus aren't...? When he said you were staying the night I didn't think he meant—''

''Of course not!'' Jenna denied quickly. ''He gave me his spare bed, that's all. He said we could both stay tonight, by the way.''

Katie regarded her fixedly for a moment longer, then shook her head slightly as though dismissing the thought as fantastic, and looked about them. ''Mmm. It's still a bit of a mess, isn't it? Just as well you did leave early yesterday.''

''Yes, the water would have done a lot more damage before anyone noticed it. The upstairs neighbors were away for the weekend.''

As if on cue there was a knock at the door, and Jenna hurried to open it, revealing embarrassed neighbors bearing apologies and a placatory gift of wine. She made sure that Katie had no more opportunity to question her about the night she'd spent at Marcus's apartment.

A couple of weeks later Mr. and Mrs. Crossan held an engagement party for Dean and Callie. Katie arranged to spend the weekend at her parents' place helping with the preparations. Casting about for an excuse not to join her, Jenna said the house would be full and anyway she had some work to get through. But of course she'd be at the party. Marcus had offered a lift.

She did sometimes bring work home from her job copy-editing documents for university staff members. It was a plausible excuse, and she made sure that Katie saw her working over a pile of papers on Friday before Dean came in his parents' car to pick up his sister.

That week Jenna had bought a new dress and spent a very expensive session with a hairdresser, who put some subtle highlights in and gave her a new, short and sassy style.

When she met Marcus at her door on Saturday night, he looked over the low-necked bright pink dress and high-heeled shoes and said, "If you want to show Dean what he's missing, that'll do it."

"It's a party," Jenna said defensively. Marcus looked terrific, she thought with mild surprise. She'd never taken much notice of what he wore, but he presented a picture of casual male elegance in a natural linen shirt, darker trousers and a light jacket.

On the journey they hardly spoke. Marcus seemed preoccupied, and Jenna was tense. On their arrival he opened the car door for her and briefly took her arm. "I'll take you home whenever you've had enough."

"I'll be fine," Jenna said, tilting her head and straightening her shoulders.

She felt an inevitable pang when Dean greeted her with a hug and a kiss on her cheek, but kept the smile on her face as she turned to Callie and handed her the gift-wrapped parcel containing a carefully chosen set of crystal wineglasses.

Callie looked radiant and Dean more handsome than ever. Jenna was glad that Marcus soon guided her away from them to get drinks. He handed her the gin and lemon she asked for, murmuring, "You'd better have something to eat too. There are nuts and dips over here." He guided her to the table.

"Don't worry." Jenna took a taco chip and dipped it in guacamole. "I won't get drunk and molest you again," she said before nibbling at the chip.

Marcus lifted a brow. "You disappoint me, Jenna. I was looking forward to it."

Her eyes widened. Was Marcus *flirting* with her?

His teasing smile said he was. Then he gave a soft laugh. "I told you I enjoyed that kiss. Is it too much to hope for a repeat performance?"

Flustered, Jenna stammered, "Yes...I mean, you know I was...I wasn't myself that night. Katie says you're like a big brother to me."

"Katie says a lot of very silly things," Marcus pronounced. He watched her take another nibble at the chip and lick at a little guacamole that had escaped. "I think I should make it clear," he said, "that I don't regard you as a sister."

Disconcerted, for a brief moment she felt hurt, then she saw his eyes momentarily shift and realized that Dean was watching them. Marcus looked back at her and inclined his head close to her ear. "If you want a smokescreen, I'm available."

Light dawned. He was pretending to be attracted by her so that Dean and anyone else with an inkling of her real feelings for him needn't think she was a discarded wallflower.

Her pride rebelled. "You don't need to do this, Marcus. Like I told you, I'm a grown-up."

"I'd have said you had a bad case of arrested development, myself."

Her eyes widening at his slightly waspish tone, she said, "What?"

"You've been in a state of suspended animation ever since Dean went to the States. When are you going to wake up and smell the flowers?"

"I haven't sat at home pining," she protested, stung by his portrayal of her languishing for love. "I've got an interesting job and plenty of friends— I've even dated a bit."

"You haven't had a serious relationship, have you?"

Astounded, Jenna snapped, "That's none of your business!"

Marcus laughed aloud, the sound deep and full-throated. It transformed his face, relaxing the seemingly harsh planes of nose and cheekbones and bringing a warmer look to his eyes. She saw Dean turn again and regard his brother curiously.

"I don't see what's funny," she hissed at Marcus.

The effort he made to control the curve of his mouth belied any implicit apology. "You just reminded me so much of the way you used to be as a kid."

"Short-tempered?" she asked suspiciously.

Marcus shook his head. "You were such a little thing, but stubborn as a baby donkey. Loyal to a fault and aggressive in defense. No one could put you down. And woe betide anyone who attacked one of the twins.''

''A little monster.''

''Not at all. The loyalty may have been misguided quite often, but it's an admirable trait, if irritating at times. And the aggression mellowed as you grew older.''

''I was pretty insecure when we arrived next door. I guess I was overcompensating.''

After her father's death, her mother's world had crumbled and she could hardly rouse herself to care for a bewildered and frightened six-year-old. Jenna's father had been a farm worker trying to save money for his own herd when the tractor he was driving rolled down a hillside and killed him.

They'd had to move out to make room for her father's replacement, and her mother had taken another cottage offered by a neighboring couple at a low rent for six months. ''Until you decide what you're going to do,'' the wife said.

They didn't realize that Karen, sunk in grief, was incapable of making decisions.

Jenna remembered the day she'd taken charge of her own life. Karen was standing with a butter knife in her hand, halfway through making Jenna's school lunch, but had apparently forgotten what she was doing.

''The school bus will be here soon,'' Jenna had told her impatiently. She'd had to go into Karen's room that morning and wake her to get breakfast. ''Mummy?''

Her mother seemed deaf. Jenna realized she was

silently crying, tears dripping down her cheeks, oblivious to everything except her own pain.

It was the loneliest moment of Jenna's short life. Lonelier than when she'd watched her father's coffin lowered into the ground and dimly, frighteningly, known she would never see him again.

She took the knife gently in her small, capable fingers and said, "It's all right, Mummy. I can do it myself."

From then on she'd got her own breakfast and lunch, whether Karen was up or not, and caught the school bus on time every day.

After the six months were up, they moved to a dispirited little town that had once had a dairy factory and was now struggling to keep any population because the factory had closed and there was no work. But rent was cheap.

There was a new school too and Jenna, starting in the middle of a term, was an outsider. She suffered loneliness and some mild bullying, learned to stand up for herself and in time made a few friends.

She patiently reminded her mother when it was time to do the washing or cook dinner, or if they needed more groceries. For two years she looked after her mother as much as her mother looked after her.

Then one day Karen looked about at where they were living as if she'd never seen it before and said, "We're moving out of here."

They'd shifted to a pleasant dormitory village where half the population commuted to Auckland every day. Where people grew roses and hibiscus and mowed the lawns every week. Mrs. Crossan welcomed them from over the fence and invited Jenna for a swim and to play with the twins.

She thought she'd loved them both from that very first day.

Chapter Four

"What's the dreamy little smile about?" Marcus's voice intruded on the memory.

"I was remembering when I met Dean and Katie." Marcus must have been there in the background too, she supposed. But she'd naturally been more interested in the twins, who were her own age.

"That accounts for it," Marcus said dryly.

She recalled only a day full of sunshine and childish laughter, playing tag across the green grass and climbing into the wide, cradling branches of the old puriri, swinging thrillingly back to earth by way of the sturdy rope that hung from it. And her mother looking almost relaxed, acting like the mother she had been two years ago, smiling as she spoke with Mrs. Crossan and watched the children splash about in the pool.

Marcus's voice interrupted again. "Losing a youthful dream isn't the end of the world. One day you'll find it doesn't hurt anymore."

"Is that how it was with you?"

When he didn't answer, frowning as though at a loss to know what she meant, she reminded him, "You told Katie your childhood sweetheart married someone else."

"Oh, that." He looked slightly rueful. "It just shows, you see. I'd completely forgotten."

"I think you made it up," she accused.

"Not at all. When I was eleven I was madly in love with a girl in my class. A plump child with apple cheeks, and braces on her teeth. I thought they were incredibly sexy."

"Sexy?" Jenna nearly choked on her drink.

"Eleven-year-old boys tend to be into hardware. Airplanes, motorbikes and girls with a mouthful of gleaming metal." He looked blandly solemn.

"Did you ever get to kiss her?"

"Hell, no. I worshipped her from afar—well, two desks away—for six months, then we left for different schools the following year and I never saw her again."

"That's sad." Jenna made her eyes big and sorrowful.

"A tragedy," Marcus agreed. "Romeo and Juliet all over again."

Jenna giggled, startled that she still remembered how to laugh. The cold leaden lump that had taken the place of her heart began to melt around the edges.

Marcus was right, she would get over her shock and secret grief. Gratefully she touched his arm. "Thanks, Marcus."

He shrugged her off, looking faintly irritated. Then, as if to make up for it, he took her hand, his fingers curving about hers in a strong clasp. "You've nothing to thank me for," he said in a rather gravelly tone. "But I'm monopolizing you. We'd better circulate."

Later in the evening Jenna was placing a platter of rock oysters garnished with lemon slices and parsley on the long supper table, when Marcus appeared at her side.

"Looks good," he commented. "Shall I save you some before they all go?"

"Thanks." Jenna threw him a smile and hurried back to the kitchen to help Katie and Mrs. Crossan.

When all the food was laid out and everyone milled about with filled plates, Marcus appeared again at her side, holding a large platter piled with savories, seafood and chicken wings.

"I thought we could share." He leaned across her to snaffle paper napkins and forks from the table. Looking about, he added, "There's nowhere to sit. Let's take it outside."

He led her into a broad passageway where a few people stood about with plates and forks. "Hold this for a minute."

Jenna stood with the loaded plate as he disappeared, to return in a few minutes with an opened bottle of wine and two glasses.

Outside, light spilled from several windows, but the perimeter of the lawn was cool and dark. Marcus made unerringly for the big old puriri tree that had been there since before the house was built.

Guessing his objective, Jenna followed. She recalled when his father had built the wooden seat around the tree. And the summer that Marcus had helped the younger ones erect a rickety tree hut in its gnarled branches. They'd used it for several years before they became too old for games and it fell to pieces.

Jenna's mother, helped by Mrs. Crossan's practical brand of sympathy, had gradually emerged from the half world she'd been living in, fighting her way back to a normal life. She'd found a job working for a publishing house, first part-time in the office and later full-time in charge of distribution. Mrs. Crossan had promised to keep an eye on Jenna after school.

Once, when Jenna was thirteen, Karen had considered moving to a shoreside suburb closer to her office in Auckland, but when she suggested it Jenna had dissolved in angry tears. All the insecurities and misery of the two years after her father's death rose to the surface in furious, door-slamming, hysterical protest. The subject was never mentioned again.

Jenna sat on the worn, smooth wood of the seat, placing the food between herself and Marcus. A breeze stirred the leaves overhead, and she rubbed at her arms.

"You're cold." Marcus stripped off his jacket and draped it around her shoulders, ignoring her protest. The satin lining was warm, and a faint woodsy aroma mingled with the smell of the fabric.

He poured wine and handed her a glass.

"What do you want?" he asked, indicating the plate.

Jenna peered down at the indeterminate mass. "I can't see what's there."

"Oyster?" He handed her a fork.

"If I can find them."

Marcus speared into the mound of food. "Open your mouth," he said.

She obeyed, and he slid the pungent morsel smoothly onto her tongue. He watched her for a moment before taking another for himself.

Her eyes becoming accustomed to the dimness, Jenna hunted for the pearly glow of the oyster shells and began to help herself. When all the oysters were gone, she had a chicken wing and a savory pastry, leaving the rest for Marcus while she sipped at the second glass of wine he'd poured for her.

"You don't eat enough," he said.

"I've just pigged out on oysters."

He made a derisory sound. "Hardly a meal."

"I'm fine."

He finished a couple more savories and wiped his fingers on one of the napkins, then put the plate aside and leaned against the puriri, draining his wine.

A moth fluttered by on pale wings and disappeared into the darkness. As Marcus topped up Jenna's glass and refilled his own, a burst of laughter floated from the house.

"Should we go back to the party?" Jenna asked.

"There's no hurry. Are you warm enough now?"

"Yes, but you..." She touched the jacket he'd given her.

"Don't worry about me."

In the house the laughter died, a gradual hush taking its place. One voice—Mr. Crossan's—was audible, followed by a round of clapping.

"They're making speeches," Jenna said. Congratulatory speeches. Dean would be expected to say something too, about his engagement, his fiancée. "You should be there." They'd be looking for him.

His hand closed over hers, checking her movement to get up. "You don't want to be there, do you?"

Jenna didn't answer, and he said, "Neither do I. Let's finish our wine."

They did so in silence punctuated distantly by Dean's friends indulging in some good-natured heckling, further laughter and applause, some raucous cheers. Then the buzz of talk began again, and unconsciously Jenna breathed a sigh of relief.

Marcus drained his glass and turned his head, took her glass from her and placed them both beside the bottle at his side. "Are you okay?" he asked.

"Yes." She stood up, so quickly that the jacket slipped from one shoulder.

Marcus got up too, made a grab for the jacket and briefly grasped her bare shoulder before he pulled the garment around her again.

He didn't immediately move away, instead standing with both hands clasping the lapels. His lips brushed her forehead, and to her dismay she felt tears well hotly in her eyes. She choked back a sob.

"Jenna," he said. His lips found a trickle of moisture on her cheek. "Don't." The admonition came out in a soft growl.

Men hated women's tears. She was embarrassing him—and herself. "S-sorry," she whispered, gritting her teeth. "Just leave me alone and I'll be all right." Closing her eyes tightly, she willed the tears away.

"I can't do that." His long fingers curved about her nape, his thumb absently moving over the skin just behind her ear.

He altered his grip, turning her face up to his. He kissed her wet eyelids, and then she felt his warm, velvety mouth on hers, parting her lips just a little, with a sureness and tenderness that was electrifying.

She made a muffled sound of surprise, and for a split second he seemed to hesitate, but then his arm came about her waist inside the shelter of his jacket, while the hand on her nape shifted, lazed down her throat and splayed across the bare flesh exposed by her low-necked dress.

Jenna's heartbeat accelerated. Heat suffused her body. Her bewildered mind was telling her this was crazy, but her body wasn't listening. It was listening instead to the steady beating of Marcus's heart against her breast, and his quickened breathing. It was inhaling the clean, masculine scent of his skin and tasting his mouth as it moved gently on hers, making the kiss deeper, more intimate, more exciting. She didn't realize she'd wound her arms around his neck until the jacket fell from her shoulders to the ground.

As the cold air played about them, she involuntarily shivered, and Marcus abruptly lifted his mouth.

He slackened his hold and put a few inches of space between them. She heard him take a long, harsh, unsteady breath.

"I didn't mean that to be quite so…enthusiastic," he said.

"I got a bit carried away myself." She felt disoriented, as though she'd stepped out of a familiar door and found herself in a foreign country. "And I didn't mean it, either."

"I'm well aware of that." He stooped and picked up the jacket, holding it out to her.

Jenna stepped back. "It's all right." She was hot all over now. "It's…uh…time we went in, anyway."

The sound he made might have been an attempt at a laugh. "More than time, I'd say." He seemed to hesitate, though. "I guess that was hardly fair."

Fair? It had been…overwhelming. And a distinct shock.

"Still," Marcus said, flinging the jacket over his shoulder and pushing a hand through his hair, "you know what they say."

"What?" She was trying to absorb what had happened here, scarcely listening.

"About love and…never mind," he said after a tiny pause. "It had the desired effect, anyway. Stopped you crying."

It had done that, all right. Jenna cleared her throat. "A bit drastic, wasn't it?"

"It was only a kiss, honey." His manner was casual now, as if a kiss—that kiss—were nothing.

For the first time she wondered just how much practice he'd had. Jenna had met some of his girlfriends. She had no idea if he'd been serious about any of them, but he was certainly much more experienced than she was, although she'd kissed a few men in her time. Maybe kisses didn't mean much to him.

"Well," she said, trying for flippancy, "you know how wine affects me. And you did ply me with drink."

"You're not drunk," he said with a hint of asperity. "If you were, I wouldn't have touched you."

He'd warned her he wanted to kiss her again. Only she'd thought that was for his brother's benefit, to make her laugh and look as though she were enjoying the party. And maybe to reassure her that she was attractive to other men.

Not that she doubted he'd enjoyed the kiss. Nor could she deny that she had, too.

Still nursing the pain of her unwanted love for Dean, how could she have responded to another man like that? Surely she wasn't that shallow?

Sex, she assured herself as they walked back to the house. She'd been deliberately keeping it in the background for four long years, and now her hormones had decided enough was enough.

And maybe they were right. She had no one to be faithful to. What reason did she have to be celibate any longer? Only her outdated principles, a romantic notion that she wanted to wait for the ultimate commitment of marriage, and innate caution.

For a second she toyed with the idea of turning to Marcus and saying, "Take me home with you. Take me to bed. Make love to me."

But of course she couldn't. It would be totally outside her normal behavior, and in the morning she'd be bound to regret it. And they were both staying here for the night, Marcus in the room he'd had as a boy, and Jenna in Katie's room. She didn't want to think about where Dean and Callie would sleep.

And, anyway, she and Marcus—impossible. She was too close to his family. How would they react if they found out? There'd be complications, repercussions. Nothing would ever be the same. She might lose the nearest thing to family that she had.

The thought stirred a faint echo of atavistic panic, similar to her feelings when her mother had suggested moving closer to the city, and later when Karen had told her she was remarrying and moving to Invercargill to be with her new husband, a publisher she'd met at a conference.

That time Jenna had hidden her feelings better, knowing it was unfair to expect her mother to forgo a second chance at happiness, when she herself expected to marry within a few years.

Karen had given Jenna the option of going with her and continuing her studies in the south, but after agonizing months of indecision, she'd chosen to stay in Auckland. She wouldn't be a third wheel in her mother's marriage.

Marcus opened the back door and switched on the light, making her blink as he closed the door behind them and looked at her narrowly.

She'd been crying, and then been very thoroughly kissed, and probably looked a fright. Raising a hand to her hair, she smoothed it behind her ear. "I need to tidy up."

She scooted by him and ran up the stairs. At the top she glanced over her shoulder and momentarily paused. Marcus was standing at the foot of the staircase, with a look on his face she had never seen before. Intent, hungry, almost predatory.

Then he smiled, and the look vanished. A trick of the light, she told herself, the angle of his head making those high cheekbones seem more prominent, his narrow nose hawklike, the gray eyes darker, deeper set. She turned away and scurried toward the bathroom.

* * *

Somehow Jenna made it through the rest of the party and even slept afterward. Maybe the wine helped.

Katie was still sprawled on her stomach with her face buried in the pillow when Jenna got up and slipped into the bathroom for a shower.

She emerged, her damp hair tousled, a large towel wrapped about her, to find Marcus lounging against the passage wall, arms folded over his bare chest. He wore nothing but a pair of black satin athletic shorts.

She'd seen him in less. They had swum together with his brother and sisters every summer for years, nor was this the first time they'd bumped into each other coming to and from the bathroom.

But she'd never really noticed that his square shoulders, narrow hips and long, lean legs were perfectly proportioned for a man, or that his arms were so muscular.

Nor had she ever felt so conscious that she too was wearing very little. The towel was large and enveloped her quite modestly, but when his eyes took in her bare shoulders and legs, although his face remained impassive, she felt her body tingle in instinctive, primitive response. Clutching the towel tighter, she was glad he couldn't see through the concealing bulk of the cloth.

Marcus straightened. "Good morning. I heard the shower stop and figured you'd be out soon."

"It's all yours," she said, sidling from the doorway.

"Thanks." He moved toward it. As she turned away he said quietly, "And…Jenna?"

Reluctantly she faced him again. "Yes?"

"Thanks for last night."

That threw her completely, bringing warmth to her cheeks. "I should be thanking you for taking pity on me."

Marcus frowned. "Is that what you think I was doing?"

"What else?"

Another door opened and Dean stumbled into the passageway. "Hi." He peered at them blearily. "Anyone in the bathroom?"

"I'm using it," Marcus told him. "I won't be long."

Jenna said brightly, "Good morning, Dean."

As Marcus entered the bathroom, Dean grunted at her and retreated again into the bedroom behind him. She heard his voice saying something indistinguishable behind the closed door as she turned toward Katie's room.

Jenna was making coffee and toast when Marcus came into the kitchen. He was the only naturally early riser in his family, and this wasn't the first time they'd shared breakfast before the others got up.

"Just like old times." Marcus echoed her thoughts as they sat at the breakfast bar. He reached for a slice of toast and spread it thickly with butter.

Jenna pushed the marmalade toward him and bit into her own toast so she'd have an excuse not to reply. This wasn't like old times, it was…different.

She watched him spoon into the marmalade and dribble some onto his toast. His hands were broad and the fingers long. A man's hands, with a few dark hairs curling about the wide silver strap of the watch on one wrist. Last night that hand had been warm on her skin while he kissed her.

Hastily she dropped her gaze to her distorted reflection on the surface of her coffee.

She hadn't really looked at Marcus since he'd been a gangling sixteen-year-old with a fuzzy dark growth on his cheeks, and limbs that seemed to have outgrown his thin body. She'd seen the changes in him then, realizing that he was turning into a grown-up, and wondered what it felt like. But she hadn't known how to ask him.

She couldn't remember noticing when the process had completed itself, the gradual transformation from skinny boy to well-built man.

By the time Jenna hit adolescence herself, he'd seemed very much an adult, one she saw less and less of as he went to university, gaining a commerce degree, then worked in England as a security guard for a year before coming back to New Zealand.

With a friend he'd set up a small factory making security gates and doors. As the business expanded they moved to bigger premises and branched into burglar alarms, locks, armored transport. The company was well-known now.

Katie had told Jenna with pride that her brother had "made his first million" some years ago. Since then his picture had been in the business pages of the newspaper more than once. He was a success.

But to her he had been simply Katie and Dean's brother.

Marcus got up with his empty cup in his hand. "More for you?"

Jenna handed him hers and watched as he refilled

them. He put hers in front of her and reseated himself. "You don't have a hangover, do you?"

She shook her head. She'd been very careful after that episode under the puriri. He was right, she had not been drunk when he kissed her, and she hadn't wanted to run the risk of being so later. If she could behave that way when she was sober, what might she do after having too much to drink?

"What are you thinking?" he asked.

"About what I've been doing with my life." She had friends she liked being with, and her job at the university was stimulating, often challenging, sometimes hectic, the pay enough to cover her half of the rent and everything she needed.

She was good at what she did, but had never been ambitious. While Marcus had been forging a business and Dean studying to further his career, and Katie climbed to the rank of supervisor in her office, Jenna had waited like Sleeping Beauty for Dean to return, a fairy-tale prince carrying her off to happy-ever-after.

Arrested development, Marcus had said. She winced inwardly. She'd put her life on hold for a stupid, adolescent delusion.

"You think I've been silly," she said.

"I never said that."

"It's true."

"We all make mistakes." He paused. "I've made some pretty major ones myself."

With exaggerated gloom Jenna said, "You're just trying to make me feel better."

He gave her one of his rare, restrained grins. "Dead right. Is it working?"

"Tell me about your mistakes."

"Uh-uh." He shook his head, then said, relenting, "I suppose not kissing Essie Ramsbottom was a mistake."

"Essie…?"

"Braces," he explained succinctly. "Now I'll never know what it would have felt like." He waited for her tiny spurt of laughter. "And I suppose," he said slowly, "kissing you was a mistake. But I can't say I regret finding out what that was like."

Jenna looked away. "Forget it," she muttered.

"Oh, I don't think so."

He was leaning back in his chair a little, one hand resting negligently on the table, the other tucked into the belt of his moleskin trousers. His jaw looked strong and uncompromising and his eyes oddly considering.

Chapter Five

A strange sensation feathered its way up Jenna's spine. It wasn't fear—of course she wasn't frightened of Marcus, that was unthinkable. But she couldn't help remembering that moment last night when she'd seen him looking up at her from the foot of the stairs. "What do you mean?" she asked cautiously.

The disconcerting expression vanished, and he leaned forward to pick up his cup, then looked at her again, and now his eyes were light and unreadable. "I try to learn from my mistakes," he said. "What about you?"

Warily she sipped her own coffee. What had she learned from four years of wasted time? That she ought not to waste any more, was the logical conclusion. "Maybe I should go away," she blurted.

"Away?" he queried sharply.

"Australia? Or Invercargill, maybe." Where her mother was.

"Running to Mummy after all?" His jaw tightened. "I thought you had more guts than that."

She said defensively, "It's just a thought. I don't need anyone to tell me what I should or shouldn't do."

"That's the girl!"

"And I'm not a girl." He'd begun to make a habit of harping on her childishness.

A gleam of sympathy lit his eyes. "No, you're a very attractive young woman, Jenna. With intelligence and grit, when you care to use them." He looked at her surprised and self-conscious expression and added, his eyes glinting wickedly, "And a sinfully sexy mouth."

She opened it, trying to think of an answer, some snappy comeback, but nothing useful came to mind. Then to her relief they heard footsteps descending the stairs and heading rapidly toward the kitchen, and Mr. Crossan came in, rubbing his hands and demanding a cup of coffee.

Despite his earlier appearance upstairs, Dean and Callie were the last to come down for breakfast, pink-cheeked and happy and slightly sleepy. Replete with love.

Don't think about it, Jenna scolded herself. And tried not to.

By lunchtime the remnants of the party were cleared away, and everyone picnicked in the kitchen. The men leaned against the counters, the women squeezed around the breakfast bar. Nobody could be bothered setting the dining table and carrying the various dishes of leftovers through.

Callie picked up a cold chicken wing and said to Jenna, "You grew up with Dean and Katie, didn't you?"

"Mmm-hmm." Jenna bit into a leftover sandwich. It had tomato in it and the bread had gone soggy.

"So you're old friends. You'd have some stories for me, I bet." Callie cast a cheeky glance at her fiancé, standing beside Marcus. "Katie's too loyal to her twin to tell tales."

Jenna swallowed, the soggy bread forming a lump in her throat. "I wouldn't dare," she said. "Dean knows too much about *my* childhood." The last thing she wanted was to be drawn into recounting Dean's youthful peccadilloes to Callie.

"Too true." Dean grinned. "No use pumping Jenna, love."

Katie said, "Ask Marcus. He was always pulling the three of us out of trouble."

"Marc?" Callie appealed to him. "What about you? My folks told Dean all the embarrassing things I ever did as a kid. They even showed him my baby pictures!"

Marcus smiled at her. "If it's baby pictures you want, I think Mum's got one of him naked on a rug."

"Ooh!" Callie rounded her eyes and mouth. "That I've got to see! Is there one of you too, Marc?"

Marcus and Dean both laughed, and Marcus shook his head.

Jenna was fighting a suffocating anger. Callie was just having fun, not flirting with Marcus. *Marc.* Jenna had never shortened his name. In fact, Dean was the only person who did.

And of course that was why Callie did it; she wouldn't know that Marcus didn't like it.

Not that he seemed at all bothered now, smiling at Callie as if they'd known each other forever. As if he didn't care what she called him so long as she smiled back at him.

Unfair, Jenna reminded herself. Marcus, like the rest of the family, wanted to make Dean's fiancée feel she belonged.

Jenna wasn't even sure why she was angry. Perhaps an oversensitivity to Dean's feelings, to any sign that Callie could possibly be interested in another man.

And Dean's feelings were none of her business.

The others were laughing, Dean protesting at the idea of their mother dragging out baby pictures, Marcus saying his were of no interest to anyone.

Jenna caught Katie's eyes, thought she saw a hint of anxiety in them, and realized she was the only one not joining in the banter. Making herself smile, Jenna turned to Callie. "I've got a picture of them both skinny-dipping," she remembered.

Katie squealed. "Oh, you've still got that? Callie, you've got to see it!"

"Little sneaks," Dean accused his sister and Jenna. "Peeping Thomasinas. Baby voyeurs."

Jenna had been given a camera for Christmas when she was twelve, the year she was invited to join the Crossans on a lakeside camping holiday. At that age Dean's mates had regarded hanging about with girls as suspicious. When he and a young friend went off for a swim with Marcus to supervise, the two girls had secretly followed, gleefully concealing themselves behind the scrubby manuka and orange-flowered flax that fringed the narrow shore at a secluded part of the lake, snapping the boys when they stripped and ran into the water naked.

Marcus was looking at Jenna, his head cocked slightly, one eyebrow lifting. She stared defiantly back at him. "I'll find it," she said, "when I get home."

She knew exactly where it was, in a camphorwood box that held her most precious possessions. Her parents' wedding photo and a picture of herself as a baby, held in her father's arms. A gold-and-pearl tiepin that had belonged to him. The wedding and engagement rings her mother had given her when she married again. Photographs of Katie and of Dean, with or without other members of his family, some with Jenna herself.

Marcus turned to tip the dregs of his coffee into the sink. She wondered if he was embarrassed at the idea of the photograph being resurrected. He'd been older than the other two, a teenager, physically developed.

Not that there was much to see in the photo. He'd had his back to the camera, but she remembered watching him shuck off his jeans, and how she'd felt herself flushing behind the camera, a strange little wiggle of guilty excitement in her stomach as he straightened and the muscles of his flanks and thighs tautened before he followed the two younger boys into the water.

Callie smiled at her mischievously. "I'll look forward to seeing it sometime."

Already Jenna regretted the rash offer.

* * *

Marcus dropped both girls off later in the day, accepting Katie's offer of a coffee.

He didn't stay long, and while Katie cleared the cups away, Jenna followed him to the hallway. "I could say I've lost that photo," she offered quietly, "if you don't want Callie to see it."

His hand on the door, he turned to look at her. "It doesn't bother me. I'm surprised you've kept it all this time."

When she didn't say anything, he gave a low laugh. "Of course, Dean's in it. How many pictures of him have you kept?"

"I've got pictures of you all." Though his guess was too close for comfort. "You must have photos of me somewhere." If he ever kept family photographs.

For an instant his eyes glazed. "I have... somewhere."

"There you are, then."

"Where are we, Jenna?" he said, his voice somehow deliberate.

She blinked, not understanding. "It was a rhetorical remark. I didn't mean anything."

His short sigh sounded impatient. "Yeah, I know. I guess it's too soon."

For what? But she didn't ask, some instinct making her keep her mouth shut.

"One day," he said with suppressed force, "you'll have to come out of that cocoon you've wrapped yourself in. It'll be interesting to see what emerges."

He opened the door and let himself out, then snapped it shut behind him, leaving her staring at the smooth, painted wood.

He hadn't even said goodbye. And he'd seemed unaccountably angry.

With her? She hadn't done anything...

She trailed back into the kitchen, scowling.

Katie turned to her from the sink and covered a yawn with her wet hand. "Early night," she said.

"Mmm. Me too. Shall I dry those?"

"Leave them to drain." Katie let the water gurgle out and dried her hands. "Are you okay, Jenna?"

Jenna swallowed an unusual urge to snarl at her friend. Her concern was wearing, but she meant well. "A bit tired, like you."

She was glad, a little later, to go to her own room and be alone at last. Wearing the big T-shirt she slept in, she slumped down on the bed, then got up and went to the secondhand rimu wardrobe that stood in a corner of the room and opened the deep drawer at the bottom.

With the camphorwood box in her hands, she climbed into bed, holding the box on her lap for a minute or two before opening it.

The bulky envelope was at the bottom. She put the box aside on the night table and sifted through the photographs in the envelope.

There it was. Two young boys in the water, thigh-deep and splashing each other, laughing. And Marcus—his dark head half-turned so that his face was in profile, his already broadening shoulders tapered to narrow flanks, his long legs fuzzed with hair.

She looked at Dean's laughing face and felt a melting, asexual fondness for the child in his innocent boyhood.

But also in her vision was Marcus, unaware of the

camera, standing tall and straight and strong. Again heat flooded her face, and guilty excitement burned as it had when she'd clicked the shutter that day. An excitement she'd put down to the fear of discovery.

This had never happened before, all the hundreds of times she'd looked at the photograph. She'd always focused her attention on Dean, cutting Marcus out of her consciousness along with the other boy, whose name she didn't even recall. As she'd cut out—buried in her subconscious—the memory of that emotion, because it embarrassed her.

She had refused to recognize it then, but she was no longer a young girl barely embarked on the journey to womanhood and alarmed at its physical manifestations. Now she knew what the feeling was. It had been there again last night, in the garden when Marcus kissed her. When she'd kissed him back. Desire.

For a couple of weeks Jenna deliberately avoided Marcus. Time to regain a sense of perspective, she hoped. To suppress newly wakened emotions that were unsettling and somehow, she sensed, dangerous.

It wasn't too difficult at first. Marcus always made himself available when his family needed him or they had a special occasion to celebrate, but he was the most self-sufficient of the siblings, and sometimes Katie didn't see him for months.

When Katie told her one evening that he'd phoned and was on his way over, Jenna said she had to return some overdue library books and planned to have supper in town with a friend from work. She quietly called the friend and made the arrangement, leaving

Katie with a cheery, "Bye. I might be late home—say hi to Marcus for me."

She hadn't seen him in sixteen days when she answered the phone and his deep, distinctive voice said, "Jenna."

"Hi," she said, and quickly added, "I'll get Katie for you."

Afterward Katie said, "I don't know why he called. It's not like Marcus to phone just to chat."

In the first weeks after Dean went overseas Marcus had been around to their new flat quite often, keeping an eye on his little sister, Jenna had guessed, in case she pined for her twin. Gradually the visits had tailed off as Katie became accustomed to Dean's absence and she and Jenna showed they could manage on their own.

Maybe he was afraid Katie was feeling left out now that Dean was engaged. Jenna herself was alert for signs of distress or disappointment. But Katie seemed fine with the situation. She talked on the telephone almost every evening to Dean and lunched with Callie while Dean was being interviewed for a job. They even arranged a girls' night out, taking in a romantic film and ending the evening with decadent desserts at an all-night café.

Katie took it for granted that Jenna would come. "And Callie will stay the night. She doesn't mind sleeping on the sofa. It's okay with you, isn't it?"

Jenna said of course it was all right. And she went along for the evening, unable to think of an excuse that wouldn't renew Katie's suspicion.

At least during the film they didn't have to talk, and at the café the music was too loud for real conversation. Back at the flat, Katie remembered Jenna's offer to show Callie the nude photo of Dean and Marcus.

"I lost it," Jenna said without even thinking about it, then felt a stab of guilt. She didn't normally lie, but it was too late now to take it back. "Sorry."

Katie looked at her rather oddly, and Callie seemed disappointed but soon got over it. She and Katie were still chatting and laughing long after Jenna went to bed.

Jenna recognized to her shame that she was jealous, and wondered if she had been subconsciously hoping that if Katie and Callie didn't get on, Dean would change his mind about marrying the American girl. She decided to stop looking for signs.

Katie wanted to spend the next weekend at her parents' home, cajoling Marcus into taking her. Jenna declined to go, saying vaguely she had things to do.

"What things?" Katie demanded.

Jenna waved a hand. "Oh...you know. Lots of things that need catching up on. Write to my mother, mend some clothes—I haven't a decent thing to wear to work on Monday. Tidy my room."

"Wash your hair?" Katie suggested dryly.

"That too." Jenna flashed her a guilty smile. "It's been a busy week at work, and I've got a bit of a headache. Much as I love you all, I just don't feel up to this."

After a moment Katie shrugged. "I suppose we're a bit much, en masse, if you're feeling under the weather. Will you be all right on your own?"

"Of course. It's just a headache, nothing major."

She swallowed some aspirin and was sitting con-

scientiously on the sofa with a little heap of mending
when she heard the discreet toot from Marcus's car
outside and Katie went bounding past her toward the
door. Marcus didn't like being kept waiting. "Bye,"
she said breathlessly.

"Give everyone my love," Jenna called. She heard
voices and the slam of the car door, but minutes later
the burr of the bell sent her to the door.

Marcus was on the tiny porch. "Katie says you're
not well," he said.

He seemed to loom over her, a bulky figure with
the lowering light behind him. She blinked up at him.
"It's only a headache."

"Is that true, or an excuse?"

Jenna sighed. "Does it matter? Actually it is true,
but it's nothing to worry about."

"Can I get you anything?"

"I've got aspirin, thanks."

He hesitated, looking as though he might argue.
"You know where we are if you need anyone."

"Sure, but I won't."

He nodded, and she stayed in the doorway until
he'd joined Katie in the car and started the engine.

Jenna was sorting through her wardrobe on Saturday afternoon when the doorbell pealed.

The bed was covered in clothes, and she had to
pick her way over a litter of shoes, boots, balled pairs
of socks and boxes of assorted junk. She brushed dust
from her loose shirt, worn over old shorts, and tried
to tuck in strands that had escaped the band she'd
hurriedly twisted round her hair.

By the time she opened the door, Marcus had his finger on the bell again.

"What are you doing here?" She had assumed that, as he had taken Katie, he too would be staying for the weekend.

"And hello to you," he returned. As she remained staring at him, he said with a hint of impatience, "Ask me in, Jenna."

She stepped back so he could come past her and shut the door. Then she led the way to the sitting room.

Turning to face him, she asked, "What do you want?"

Marcus seemed to be looking at her with unusual attention, focusing on her face as if he needed to read something there. "A drink would be nice," he answered her. "You look all right. How's the headache?"

"Gone. Coffee, beer, lemonade? The only choices we have, I'm afraid."

He opted for beer and followed her into the kitchen. She made herself a shandy to keep him company, and they went back to the other room. "Did Katie send you?" she asked.

"No."

He waited for her to sit on one of the mismatched easy chairs before he took a seat on the sofa.

Jenna found she was tongue-tied, and Marcus was in no hurry to start a conversation, sipping his beer and wiping a line of froth from his upper lip without even looking at her.

When he did, his gaze seemed critical. "Katie thinks you're losing weight."

Under the baggy shirt he wouldn't have been able to tell, but his scrutiny made her self-conscious.

"Not much. I've been working hard."

She'd been keeping herself busy, trying not to leave too much time for thinking—for regrets. And hiding her feelings from Katie, maybe not altogether successfully.

"There are other ways of forgetting," Marcus said, "besides working yourself into the ground. More pleasant ways."

"I don't think hitting the bottle did me much good."

"I wasn't thinking of that."

His eyes held something that to her intense chagrin made her blush. She thought of claiming she didn't know what he meant, but he'd see through that instantly.

Fortunately he didn't appear to expect an answer. He got up, and Jenna tensed, but he walked away from her toward the window, looked out as though searching for something to interest him, then turned, his half-full beer glass held in one strong hand.

She noticed that his knuckles were white, but his face seemed emotionless. He gulped some more beer. His throat was taut and lightly tanned, the Adam's apple not prominent, but she saw it move as he swallowed.

Lowering the glass, he said, "You've never thought of any man but Dean, have you?"

"Not seriously." She had found other men fleetingly attractive, but she'd regarded herself as taken. So none of those attractions had come to anything— because she hadn't let them.

"You can't have him," Marcus said.

It was brutal, and unlike him. She felt herself pale. Her head lifted. "You don't need to remind me." It wasn't as if she'd tried to take Dean away from Callie. She'd actually bent over backward not to hint at her pain and disappointment.

"So is there anyone else on the horizon?"

Jenna's eyes widened. "There's hardly been time for that!"

"You do know other young men."

"Of course I do. Friends."

"Friends can become lovers."

"I don't need a lover!"

Marcus's mouth moved in a strange smile. The glint in his eyes made her uneasy, sending a weird little hot shiver up her spine. "Are you sure? You could have fooled me," he said, "the night of the party."

She recalled that in a moment of temporary insanity she'd thought of asking him to take her home, take her to his bed. Maybe he'd guessed. "I shouldn't have had so much wine."

He finished his drink in one movement. "But perhaps you need a friend more, right now."

"I'm certainly not ready for...for anything else!"

Marcus came closer to put his glass down on the coffee table in front of her, finding a clear space among the magazines and junk mail, beside a saucer crumbed with the remains of potato crisps. Straightening, he shoved his hands into the pockets of his dark trousers, regarding her narrowly.

"Do you always react like that to a couple of glasses of wine?"

"Throwing myself at the nearest male? No. And I wish you wouldn't keep bringing it up!"

He lowered himself again to the sofa, smiling at her now, disarming her completely. "I don't mean to give you a hard time," he said. "We've known each other so long, Jenna, I hate to see you unhappy."

"As you told me," she said, trying to believe it, "I'll get over it."

"Then let me help."

"How?" she asked starkly. "What can you do?"

"I can give you a social life apart from my family, for a start."

"I have other friends."

"Mostly they're Katie's friends too, aren't they?"

"Yes." Even people they met separately tended to become mutual friends. They liked the same people.

Marcus nodded. "And Katie will bring Dean and Callie into that circle. You need to break out of it if you're ever going to live your own life."

Jenna protested, "I'm not dependent on your family for everything." She had even dated occasionally, mainly because when Katie was dating someone she worried about Jenna sitting at home on her own.

"It wouldn't hurt to broaden your horizon."

"You think I'm narrow and dull." Indignation stirred.

Marcus laughed. "Not at all. But I think there's a world out there you haven't even begun to explore. And I'd like to show it to you."

Maybe her doubts showed. "Come on, Jenna," he urged. "What have you got to lose?"

"Why are you doing this?" she asked. "What's in it for you?"

He gave her a long, assessing look that held a germ of exasperation. "I'm helping out a friend," he said. "And I think it could be...rewarding."

"I never had you pegged as a do-gooder."

His brows shot up. "I'm not looking for a halo. Something much more...temporal."

"Like what?"

A different smile lurked in his eyes. "Let's take it one step at a time, shall we?"

Jenna moved restlessly and gulped down what was left of her shandy. A faint stirring of something curiously like anticipation shivered through her. After all, what did she have to lose? Except time spent moping around wishing for what might have been. Self-pity had never appealed to her. "All right," she said recklessly. "Let's."

He didn't move, but she had the impression he'd just released a pent-up breath. "Good," he said. "What would you like to do tonight?"

"Tonight?"

"A film...a show...dinner? What about a comedy club? You could do with a good laugh."

"I suppose," she said, lifting a shoulder. Already she had cold feet. More strongly she said, "Yes. That sounds like fun."

He stood up. "I'll pick you up around seven."

She trailed him to the door, where he turned to face her. He lifted a hand and just touched her cheek with his thumb. "Don't look so worried," he admonished. "It will be all right, I promise."

The silly thing was, Jenna thought as she closed the door after him, she believed him.

*   *   *

She did have a good laugh. Not all of the acts were truly funny, but there were enough humorous one-liners and witty monologues to keep the audience amused most of the time. She had never seen Marcus laugh so often.

Afterward they had a snack and a drink and then he delivered her home, leaving her at the door with a swift peck on her cheek. "I'm picking up Katie from home tomorrow," he said. "I don't suppose you want to come?"

"No." It was a relief to be frank, even blunt. She didn't want to see Dean with Callie again, to have to pretend it didn't matter. With Marcus she didn't need to put up a smokescreen.

"I didn't think so," he said. "I'll be in touch."

He was, less than a week later. When Katie handed her the phone and said, "Big brother wants to talk to you," Jenna tried to appear nonchalant.

A friend had loaned him a yacht for the weekend, he said, and he planned to spend a couple of days cruising about the Hauraki Gulf. "I'd like you to come."

"Just me?" Jenna asked involuntarily.

It was a moment before he answered. "You know what a poor sailor Katie is."

While still at university he'd bought, for what he said was a "single verse rather than a song," a small boat of his own, run-down and shabby. He'd spent every weekend he could spare from studying on scraping, repairing and restoring it, with occasional assistance from his younger siblings and Jenna.

Dean and Jenna had learned to help sail the boat

and loved it, but Katie spent most of the time hanging over the side until Marcus took pity and returned her to dry land. She never did acquire sea legs, and after several attempts had given up. Marcus sold the boat when he went overseas.

"He's got a boat for the weekend," Jenna relayed to Katie when she had hung up. "He needs someone to crew for him."

Katie shuddered. "No wonder he wanted to talk to you."

They left on Saturday morning, a perfect day, with a brisk breeze that filled the sails and scattered the few ragged clouds hanging over Rangitoto, the island volcano in the gulf.

The clear air, the wind in her hair, the water hissing under the hull as they skimmed the jade-green surface were wonderful fresheners. Scrambling to adjust the sails, taking a turn at the tiller, obeying Marcus's crisp, decisive orders, Jenna felt more alive than she had in weeks—maybe years.

When they anchored in a sheltered bay in the lee of a hillocky island, where woolly white sheep fled across close-shorn green paddocks, she was aching and sunburned but almost happy.

They swam in cool, clear water, Marcus in a fast crawl away from the boat and back again, while Jenna floated lazily on the surface and occasionally dived to the sandy bottom. Shell fragments glistened red, orange and pale gold on the sea bed, and tiny shimmering fish darted away from the human intruders and from a hungry gannet plummeting with folded wings into the sea. Afterward Jenna roughly dried her hair, then wrapped the towel about her waist over her swimsuit. Marcus had stripped to a pair of shorts.

"You're burned," he said, running a finger across her bared shoulders. The salt water drying on them stung. "Hang on a minute."

He disappeared below and came back with a pink plastic bottle, unscrewing the cap. "You should use more sunscreen," he scolded, turning her with a hand on her arm.

"I thought I'd used plenty." And he'd made sure she wore a hat all day, even clamping it more firmly to her head when the breeze had threatened to blow it away.

"This should help."

She shuddered as cold moisture hit her hot skin. Then his hand was smoothing it across the bones, down her arm, onto her back where her skimpy top had bared it to the merciless rays.

He anointed the other shoulder, his palm moving hypnotically over her skin. It was both soothing and disturbing. Another shiver passed over her body.

"Turn around," he said.

She did, and their eyes met before he dropped his gaze. She felt her breasts peak under the flimsy cloth covering them, and held her breath.

"Here," he said, passing her the bottle. "You can do your front."

She took the bottle from him, and he stepped away.

"Hungry?" he asked.

She was ravenous, Jenna realized, smoothing lotion down to the top of her swimsuit. The pulse in her throat was jumping. She breathed out carefully, steadying her nerves. "I could probably eat one of those sheep," she told him, "if there's no horse available."

Marcus laughed, and the tension eased. "We wouldn't be popular. I don't think we're allowed to light fires on the beach, either, but we could grill some chops and sausages in the galley and eat on deck."

While he cooked the meat, Jenna made a salad and sliced bread. Marcus found glasses and took out a bottle of wine that he'd chilled in the compact fridge.

Jenna eyed the glass he handed her as they sat on the gently rocking deck, watching a distant sunset wash the sky a pale pink and set the sea shimmering with golden light.

"I promise I won't get you drunk," Marcus said. "You should know by now I prefer my women to know what they're doing."

"Your women?"

He glanced at her, his eyes crinkling. "Figure of speech."

"I'm your crew," she reminded him.

He smiled. "I don't get my crew drunk, either. Bad for discipline."

"Are there…have there been many women?" She shouldn't ask, but the words were out before she thought better of them. "I mean—"

"I know what you meant." He seemed to consider the question, and she wondered if he was doing the mental arithmetic. "Very few, as a matter of fact," he said, and looked at her. "Do you want an exact figure?"

"No," she disclaimed. "I don't know why I asked, I shouldn't have—"

"Because you wanted to know."

He almost seemed to be pleased about it. He picked up his fork and said, pointing to her steak, "Eat that before it gets cold."

Chapter Six

They lay at anchor overnight, sleeping in narrow bunks only a few feet from each other across the width of the cabin. Marcus sent Jenna down first, descending himself twenty minutes later, by which time she had slid into her sleeping bag.

"Want the light left on?" he asked.

"No. I don't mind if you do, though."

He shot her a teasing look, and she added hastily, "I mean, if you want to read or something."

He switched it off, and she heard him undress in the dark, and the bunk creaking faintly under his weight.

"Good day?" he said quietly.

"Yes," Jenna answered. "Thank you, Marcus."

The bunk creaked again as he shifted his weight. "You don't need to thank me. I've had a great day, and I'm looking forward to tomorrow."

Maybe Marcus needed a break too. Once Katie had

asked him why he didn't take more time off, and he'd told her that no one stayed at the top by slacking. Besides, he enjoyed being "hands on" rather than leaving the running of the business to someone else.

After an early breakfast they sailed out of the cove. Jenna wore a T-shirt to ensure that the burn didn't get worse, and Marcus made sure she used sunblock every hour. He'd insisted on applying more salve on her back while she held a towel around herself before she dressed.

When they anchored for lunch he took out the pink bottle again and said, "Take off your shirt."

"I'm not wearing anything under it!" Jenna protested. Her bra straps would have irritated the tender skin.

The only visible craft was a sailboat cruising near the horizon. Marcus glanced at it and cast her a quizzical look. "You hold the front," he said patiently, "while I get some of this stuff on your back."

She was being prudish, but he hadn't seen her topless since she was ten. She probably felt more shy with Marcus than she might have with a total stranger.

Jenna crossed her arms under her breasts while he pushed the shirt up and over her shoulders. The cold splash of the lotion made her flinch, and he said, "Sorry."

"No," she said. "It feels wonderful."

Marcus laughed quietly, smoothing the cool liquid slowly into her skin. He paused to get some more, then his hand cupped one shoulder, shaping it to his moistened palm. "Considering that you have a picture of me in the nuddy," he said, "I feel I'm being short-changed here."

"We were kids." She and Katie had been, anyway.

He didn't answer, gently massaging her shoulder, his palm gliding over the heated flesh.

Jenna closed her eyes. He applied the stuff to the other shoulder, then ran his hand across her back again. For a moment it rested there, his fingers spread between her shoulder blades. The sun was warm on her bent head, and she heard the slap-slap of the water against the boat, and the soft sound of Marcus's breath as it stirred the tendrils of hair at the nape of her neck.

She felt his lips briefly touch the skin just behind her ear, and it electrified her whole body.

Then he removed his hand, saying briskly, "There you are," and pulled down the shirt.

By the time Jenna had adjusted the shirt and turned around, he had his back to her while he put the bottle of lotion away.

When he returned her to the flat, it was getting dark. Katie met them at the door and insisted on Marcus coming in for a meal.

After they'd eaten they sat around the table with a bottle of wine, and then coffee, talking. It was quite late before Marcus pushed back his chair and said he'd better be going.

Jenna yawned and began to get up too, wincing when her sore shoulder rubbed against the chair back.

"What's the matter?" Katie queried.

"A bit of sunburn."

Marcus said, "Have you got something for it here?"

"Yes, calamine," Jenna said.

"Get Katie to help you." He turned to his sister. "She needs someone to do her back."

Katie did it for her before they went to bed, and again the following morning. Marcus phoned Jenna in the evening. "How's the burn?"

"Settling down nicely. It was worth it."

He laughed. "Want to try it again?"

"Sunburn?" she parried.

"You know what I mean."

"Sailing?"

"Not necessarily."

When she didn't answer, he said with slight impatience, "A date, Jenna."

He hadn't used the word before.

"What did you have in mind?"

"If you're free we could go to a movie tomorrow evening." He paused. "Bring Katie along if you like."

Katie, who had handed the phone to her when Marcus asked for Jenna, gave her a surprised look when she relayed the invitation.

"I forgot to tell you. Dean and Callie are coming over," she said. "Dean's got another job interview, and Callie's going to look for a place for them to live in the city, so they're coming for dinner afterward. But there's no reason you shouldn't go," she added. "Have a good time."

When Marcus brought her home after the film, he glanced at the familiar car parked in front of his, and said, "Do you want me to come in with you?"

"I'm sure Dean and Callie would like to see you."

She waited for him to close the door. ''Did you know they were going to be here tonight?''

''Should I have?'' His hand at her waist urged her toward the flat.

''I just wondered,'' she said, ''if you'd invited me out tonight to be kind.''

They stopped on the porch. It was dark, the streetlight not reaching there. ''I asked you out because I wanted to spend time with you!'' he said rather forcefully. ''I hope you accepted for the same reason.''

''Of course I did,'' she said quickly. ''I mean, I enjoy doing things with you, Marcus.''

''I'm glad to hear that. And it's mutual. So...let's have no more of this stuff about you being some kind of personal charity of mine.''

Inside the flat Dean had his arm about Callie on the sofa, while Katie sprawled across one of the big old armchairs.

The greetings over, Jenna poured coffee for herself and Marcus. He gave the other chair to her before perching on the wide arm, his hand resting behind her.

''How was the job interview?'' Jenna asked Dean.

''I think it's in the bag.'' He looked pleased with himself. ''And Callie found a great apartment today. If I get this job we can afford the rent.''

Katie said, ''Have you set a wedding date?''

''Not yet.'' Dean glanced at his fiancée. ''Callie wants her parents here for it.''

Marcus looked from him to Callie. ''Of course she does.''

''There's no hurry,'' Callie said.

They chatted for a while, and then Dean made a

reluctant move. Marcus got up too, and as they were leaving Callie said brightly, "Why don't we all go out together sometime? The five of us."

Dean and Katie agreed in chorus, "Good idea." Marcus lifted an eyebrow at Jenna.

She managed a smile. "That sounds like fun."

"Marcus?" Katie turned to him.

"We'd enjoy that." Casually he hooked his arm about Jenna.

She saw Dean's look of surprise, and Katie's eyes flicking from her to Marcus.

"Dean?" Callie prompted.

"Sure." He dragged his eyes from his brother.

Marcus loosened his hold and kissed Jenna quickly on her mouth. "Good night." His wave included Katie before he turned away to follow the other two out.

When Katie shut the door and turned, obviously bursting with curiosity, Jenna shrugged and answered the unspoken question. "We're...friends. I suppose we're sort of dating," she mumbled.

"What happened on that yachting weekend?" Katie demanded.

"Nothing! Honestly."

Katie looked fascinated. "You know, I sometimes thought Marcus kind of fancied you, after he came back from overseas. He used to look at you a lot when he thought no one was watching. But I asked him once, and he just laughed and reminded me you were the same age as me, as if it had never crossed his mind that you weren't his sister. And you never said anything...you would have, wouldn't you? I mean, if he'd made a move..."

"He didn't. We're friends," Jenna repeated. That

was what he'd said, wasn't it? That she needed a
friend.

"Sure." Katie was unconvinced. "Okay."

They all celebrated Dean's job acceptance with
dinner at a Turkish restaurant that Katie had discovered when she was dating her last boyfriend.

Instead of chairs, they were seated on a low, curved
divan. Katie and Callie giggled as they arranged
themselves against the piled silk and velvet cushions,
and Callie pulled Dean down beside her. "This is
wonderful," she said. "So-o over the top."

"They have belly dancers later," Katie told her.
"The men will enjoy that."

They ordered exotic dishes and shared, sampling
each other's and making recommendations.

Marcus offered Jenna something dark and prune-
like, holding it by one end between his thumb and
forefinger.

"What is it?"

"I've no idea, but it's good. Maybe a fig?" He
slipped it between her lips and it was, as he'd said,
very good, sweet and syrupy. Marcus watched her,
and unexpectedly reached out and ran his thumb over
her lower lip, leaving a trace of the syrup before he
withdrew.

Instinctively Jenna licked at the sticky sweetness.
Her eyes locked with his, and a jolt of sexual awareness coursed through her, leaving her breathless and
dizzy.

Marcus's eyes had darkened, and she could see a
tiny muscle twitch near his jaw. Then he smiled and,
without taking his eyes from her, snaked his arm

along the padded back of the couch, letting it lie there, his fingers just touching her shoulder.

"Nice?" he said softly.

Jenna couldn't speak, managing a jerky nod instead, and some sort of smile. That light touch scorched. She couldn't recall ever being so acutely aware of another human being. When his thigh brushed against hers she bit down hard on her lip.

This is Marcus, she said to herself, dazed. *Marcus.* She'd never felt like this about him—about anyone, even Dean.

He'd already turned away, finding another delicacy to tempt her with. This time she forced herself to laugh and shake her head. "I'll feed myself, thanks. I feel decadent enough as it is."

Marcus slanted her a smile. A knowing smile, as if he knew what he'd done to her. He turned to the table but didn't take away his arm, and when the lights dimmed and a burst of music announced that the dancers were about to begin, he sank back on the cushions and closed his hand over her shoulder, bringing her into the curve of his arm.

She glanced at him a couple of times while three women in their glitter and draperies gyrated and twisted and twirled. When one of them caught his eye and danced closer, her stomach muscles rippling amazingly, he gave her a coolly amused smile. But most of the time he watched with detached interest. Katie and Callie were both teasing Dean, whispering comments while he pretended drooling fascination.

Afterward Marcus took Jenna and Katie home, declining Katie's invitation to come in. She nipped inside, leaving the door almost closed, and Marcus gave a low laugh. "My little sister trying to be tactful."

"I told her we're just friends." Jenna was flustered.

"Did you, now?"

"You said…"

"I know what I said." He put a hand on her arm and made her face him. "But one day," he said with deliberation, "I intend to make love to you, Jenna."

Her breath stopped. The change of pace was too sudden. "You're taking a lot for granted, aren't you?" She'd stepped on a nice safe merry-go-round, and it had turned into a switchback railway. Hearing the panic in her tone, she brought it down half an octave. "I never said I'd sleep with you! I don't know if I want to!"

"There's no rush." He moved his hand to tip her chin and make her look at him. "What's the problem?"

"One step at a time," she reminded him frantically.

He looked at her consideringly. "Yes. Which implies moving forward. I'm a patient man, Jenna. More so than you know, but I won't mark time forever. Living on hopes and dreams isn't my style."

Without waiting for a reply he pressed his lips briefly to hers, and then he was gone.

Katie had a new boyfriend. When Dean and Callie moved into their flat and threw a housewarming party, Jason drove the two girls along to it, although Marcus had offered.

He was there, of course, and so were his parents.

Jenna knew most of the people present and was able to give a passable imitation of enjoying herself.

The guests milled about in every room and on the small deck and lawn outside, and some were dancing in the living room, which was almost devoid of furniture. Dean and Callie still had to get around to acquiring some.

Halfway through the evening, while Jenna was chatting with Mr. and Mrs. Crossan and Marcus had gone to get drinks for the two women, the phone rang and Callie disappeared into the bedroom to talk with her parents.

Dean, his eyes bright and cheeks flushed, appeared at Jenna's side. "My fiancée's deserted me temporarily," he said. "Dance with me, Jenna."

Giving her no chance to refuse, he put his arm about her and urged her in among the dancers. "Enjoying yourself?" he asked her.

Jenna smiled widely. "It's a great party." The other guests obviously thought so.

"What gives with you and old Marc?"

"What's Katie been telling you?"

His grin teased. "She thinks there's something going on."

"What's it to you?" she asked involuntarily.

He grinned. "I guess I just want everyone I love to be as happy as I am."

Jenna made her voice sound light. "That's nice."

"I'm a nice guy," he said modestly, and moved in, twirling her exuberantly, retaining his hold on her hand when they faced each other again. "Aren't I?"

He was, she knew that. Blind to a lot of things, but nice. He deserved his happiness. For the first time she felt genuinely glad for him, a rush of affection burying her hurt. "You're really in love with Callie, aren't you?"

Foolish question, but Dean didn't seem to mind. "I'm crazy for her," he said simply. He put his hands on Jenna's waist, moving gently to the music. Suddenly sober, he said, "Thank you, Jenna, for sending me to America."

Jenna blinked. "Me? Sending you?"

"You were right, it was too good a chance to pass up. Not that I ever thought I'd meet someone like Callie." He gave her a lopsided, almost embarrassed smile. "Remember when we were kids and we said we'd marry each other?"

A lump in her throat, Jenna nodded.

"You were the first girl I ever kissed."

"You were the first boy..."

"Yeah, I know. Y'know, while we were at university I wondered sometimes if we'd end up together after all. But...obviously you weren't thinking along the same lines."

Jenna's mouth opened. "O-obviously?"

"You were dead keen for me to take the scholarship. Well," he added as if it were self-evident, "you'd never have let me go away for four years if you were serious about me." He grinned again. "I can hardly bear to be without Callie for four minutes!"

An exaggeration, she was sure, but when Callie emerged from the bedroom a few minutes later looking pink-eyed, Dean excused himself, went straight to her and gave her a hug.

Still dazed from the irony of his revelations, Jenna

rejoined the elder Crossans. Marcus handed over the drink he'd fetched for her, and for the rest of the evening stayed at her side. Around midnight, after his parents had departed, he suggested, "I'll drive you home whenever you're ready. Katie looks as though she's happy to stay on until dawn."

Katie was energetically dancing with her handsome, laughing partner. Watching them, Marcus said, "What do you think of this guy Jason?"

"He seems nice. They have the same sense of humor, but they hardly know each other yet. He was nervous about meeting her family." They'd been joking about it in the car.

"Are we so formidable?" Marcus looked across the room at his parents.

"*You* are," Jenna said involuntarily. "I think as kids the twins and I were more afraid of you than we were of your parents."

He looked at her with skepticism. "I never lifted a finger to any of you."

She shook her head. "No, only you were bigger and...somehow you always seemed..."

"Bossy?" he suggested wryly.

Jenna laughed. "I know we said so. You felt responsible for us, didn't you? Protective."

"You were so much younger." He looked rueful.

"But we're all adults now." She looked again at Katie.

Marcus did too, and then back at Jenna, his gaze disconcertingly level.

Something about that straight look disturbed her equilibrium. Her eyelids fluttered, and she had to make an effort to meet his gaze.

"That's what I'm hoping." Marcus lifted the glass in his hand and tossed off his drink. She was already holding an empty glass. "Let's dance," he said abruptly, taking her glass to deposit it with his on the nearest flat surface.

Someone had turned up the volume on the stereo system, and the noise level had risen to where people having a conversation had to stand close or shout above the music to be heard.

But as he took her hand to lead her in among the couples wiggling their hips and stamping their feet in the center of the room, the track came to an end and was replaced by a slow, dreamy number.

A few people stopped dancing and went to refresh their drinks, but the others wrapped their arms about each other and began swaying to the new rhythm.

Marcus's arms came about her, and automatically she rested her hands on his shoulders. She lifted her face and found him looking at her almost somberly, his eyes very dark and enigmatic.

They stared at each other for a long moment, swaying in time to the music, their feet hardly moving. Then he shifted his grip and brought her closer, his hands sliding to her hips, his shaven cheek rasping gently at the tender skin of her temple.

She wondered if he could feel the hurrying pulse there, and if her scent was as alluring to him as his was to her. He smelled male and exciting, under the soap and clean clothing.

When the music picked up a faster beat and the other couples broke apart, he didn't release her. Instead he said in her ear, "Shall I take you home?"

A rush of panic made her stiffen. She pulled away,

not looking at him. "If you've had enough of the party I'd appreciate a lift, thanks."

Coward, sneered a tiny voice inside her head. She tried to ignore it.

"Fine," Marcus said, his voice clipped. When she dared peek at him his face was rigidly controlled.

Outside it was cooler. She had worn a thin dress, and she hugged herself as they hurried to Marcus's car.

"Didn't you bring a jacket?" he asked her.

"I didn't think it would turn cold. I'm all right, it's warmer in the car."

It was only a ten-minute drive, and he didn't speak again until he drew up at the flat and accompanied her to the door.

He followed her into darkness, and she fumbled for the hall light and switched it on while he closed the door. "It's late," she said.

"Not too late." As she started down the passageway his hand on her arm stopped her, turned her to face him. "What are you scared of?"

"I'm not scared."

Marcus gave a short, unexpected laugh. "What you always declared when Dean dared you to do some silly, dangerous prank. I'm surprised you survived childhood." He paused, but she was staring stubbornly at the open neck of his casual shirt.

"Look at me, Jenna."

She pulled a careful breath in through her nose and looked up into his eyes. They were steady and searching and stern.

Jenna swallowed, and when she spoke her voice came out husky. "What do you want, Marcus?"

His lips curved very slightly. "If you're really an adult, not a little girl any longer, surely you know."

She felt her eyes go wider at his blunt challenge. But she didn't trust her own reactions to him. They were too new, and too disturbing. Surely unreal. "A woman who's been in love with a man for years can't just *not* be in a matter of weeks, even if she's…in lust with someone else." She might as well admit it. He must know, anyway.

"In lust?" His tone was peculiar. "Is that what you call it?"

Pulling away from him, she said, "You're an attractive man, Marcus, you must know that."

"Thank you. Then why do I hear a *but* coming?"

Difficult to express her conflicted feelings of physical fascination and emotional rejection, her muddled thoughts. "You're the nearest I've ever had to an elder brother."

"I'm not your brother!"

He'd stepped out of the role, and it unsettled her.

Until recently she had known what place each of the Crossans held in her life, and where she stood in theirs. Since Dean had brought Callie home, all those relationships had radically altered. Jenna no longer held the position in his heart that she had always imagined. Katie was growing closer to her future sister-in-law, with the inevitable consequence that Jenna sometimes felt left out. Jenna herself had withdrawn from the family circle to some extent, not being a natural masochist. And now Marcus wanted to be her lover.

"Everything's changing," she muttered, reluctant to admit how much it frightened her, throwing her back into childhood nightmares where people she loved abruptly disappeared or turned away from her, and familiarity turned to strangeness and loss.

"That's what life is about, Jenna," Marcus said patiently. "Things change. You can't lock yourself away from it, a lone princess pining in her tower. People move on, they leave the past behind, take chances and accept risks, forge new relationships. Make love."

"But I don't want—"

"You do!" He took a step toward her, and she involuntarily moved back. Then she found herself trapped against the wall, with Marcus standing over her, his hands flattened on either side of her while his eyes held hers in thrall. "You do *want*," he repeated. "You just admitted you want me."

"Don't bully me, Marcus!"

He wasn't touching her. "I'm trying to shake you awake, Sleeping Beauty. Fighting through the thorny hedge you've grown around your dreams. Tell me, has Dean ever even kissed you?"

"Yes, he has!" she claimed hotly, his weary, contemptuous tone sparking her temper. "Lots of times."

The first had been a clumsy adolescent experiment when they were both thirteen, resulting in more embarrassment than pleasure. The last was lingering and tender and poignant, before he went away.

She supposed that what she had seen as a pledge, he'd known was a goodbye to young love, because realistically the scarcely budding romantic component of their almost lifelong relationship wouldn't survive four years of separation.

Marcus's jaw tautened. She thought, and it gave

her a perverse satisfaction, that he'd received a small shock. "You've never slept with him," he said flatly.

How would he know? She gave him a silent, stubborn look, and his eyes narrowed, speculating.

He said softly, "You've never slept with anyone, have you?"

"You don't expect me to answer that!"

Unforgivably Marcus laughed. "You don't need to, little virgin," he taunted her. "It's written all over you." His voice altered to a kinder tone. "Maybe I should have taken that into account. But if you've been saving yourself for Dean, what are you going to do now?"

"I'm not going to sleep with the first man who offers!" Jenna flashed.

His mouth thinned. "I haven't suggested that."

"You said you wanted to have sex with me."

He looked as though he was going to deny it. She wondered if he was going to tell her no, she'd got it wrong.

"I want to make love with you," he said slowly, at last. "And you want it too."

"I don't love you!" she cried. "Not in the way I love—loved Dean." This wasn't love, this tug of desire, of physical need, that sometimes shook her to her core. It was too elemental. Too scary. She thrust that thought away, not wanting to examine the implications.

Marcus went lynx-eyed. "Past tense," he insisted, "or present? Let it go, Jenna. Dean's committed to Callie. He's madly, deeply in love with her."

"I know!" There was anguish in her voice. "I accept that."

"Then why can't you accept this?" he demanded, and hauled her into his arms.

Chapter Seven

It was in a strange way both like and unlike the other times Marcus had kissed her. The same rush of pleasure, unexpected and overwhelming, invaded her body.

But there was another element in the erotic charge of his lips forcing hers apart—a ruthlessness that was new and alarming, as if he were determined to blot everything else from her mind, her heart.

Her head fell back, and he shifted one arm so that he held her securely in the curve of his shoulder.

He seemed intent on demonstrating to her an unleashed sexuality, freed from the consideration and tenderness he'd shown her previously.

Not that he hurt her, he was far too skillful for that—but this was no gentle caress of comfort, no restrained if passionate exploration. It was a no-holds-barred, primal sexual revelation. A brazen assault on her senses.

At first she was shocked, as much by her own instant response as by the power of his arms holding her and the near-aggression of his kiss.

Fire licked through her veins, setting her alight, and as his complete lack of inhibition transferred itself to her, she kissed him back recklessly, her mouth as hungry and seeking as his, wanting the taste of him, arching her body over his arm at her waist, letting him take her with him to another plane of intense arousal.

She clung to his shoulders, the taut muscles bunching under her hands.

He pushed her to the wall, and his hands were on her breasts, shamelessly possessive. Her body was no longer her own, but an instrument of pleasure brought humming to life by his hands and his mouth, strung so tightly that when his fingers found a way inside her dress and touched bare skin she shivered with delight.

Marcus lifted his mouth then, his breathing harsh. "Jenna," he muttered, "this is torture. We need a bed."

Oh, yes! her mind said, before he eased away from her, leaving a cold gap between them. He still had a hand on her breast, the other resting on her hip.

Outside a car door slammed, and Jenna stiffened, pushing away his hands, turning her horrified gaze toward the door.

Katie?

Quick footsteps, and the door of the adjoining flat opened and closed. Jenna slumped with relief, and Marcus gave a smothered, unsteady laugh. He reached for her again, but she evaded him, turning blindly to enter the living room, fumbling for the light. It dazzled her eyes, the room swimming before her.

When he followed, she whirled to face him, and his eyes, dark and glittery, went to the bodice of her dress. The neckline was half off her shoulder, the lace of her bra showing.

Hastily Jenna pulled her dress into place, and ran her tongue over throbbing lips. She felt disheveled and disoriented, tiny shudders like miniature aftershocks attacking her.

Marcus moved toward her, and she stepped back with a wary little shake of her head.

His face became shuttered. He stopped inches from her, and they stared wordlessly at each other.

His mouth twisted. "I suppose it was too much to expect the walls would tumble so easily."

"You're not *that* irresistible." Jenna felt a need to attack while she gathered some kind of defenses. He was a formidable opponent, and he didn't play fair. Bewildered, she realized she was thinking of him as the enemy. Marcus, her friend—her protective, slightly bossy, almost-big-brother. Until now.

The sound he made wasn't quite a laugh. "I think I proved my point, at least."

He'd certainly proven that he could make her want him—make her almost fall into bed with him. A myriad of thoughts, half thoughts, chased each other through her mind. And a formless, barely acknowledged fear that she couldn't name or understand.

Distractedly, she thrust her fingers into her hair in a useless attempt at tidying it. Making a decision to give up Dean and her dreams of a future with him was one thing. Having a steamy affair with his brother on the rebound was something else entirely. She couldn't trust these bewildering new emotions at all. Aloud she said, "This can't be real!"

Marcus's hands lifted, then fell to his sides. "It felt real to me. More real than your girlish romantic fixation on my brother."

That was cruel. She turned away from him, swallowing hurt. The coffee table as usual was a mess. Like her life, she thought, suddenly irritated. They really ought to tidy up.

Marcus said, "I don't mean to hurt you, Jenna. But I'm getting a little tired of waiting for you to emerge from your cozy dream world."

She faced him then, her eyes hot. "You think I'm a fool. But I'm not so stupid or so juvenile that I don't know the difference between love and…lust."

He just looked at her for a moment, then he laughed. "Lust?" he echoed harshly. "That's the second time you've said that. I suppose it was lust that made you kiss me just now as if your whole life depended on it."

Jenna shrugged, looking away and down.

A hard hand came under her chin and forced it up. "Maybe I don't care. Whatever it was, it's pretty potent. You lit up for me like a Roman candle."

"Fireworks don't last," she said. "They're all flash and burn and then…ashes." She pushed his hand away, but he grabbed at her wrist and held it.

"*That's* what you're afraid of? That it might all turn to ashes?"

"It's bound to eventually," she reasoned. "Isn't it?" All his other girlfriends had disappeared from his life, hardly impinging on his family, seldom mentioned. Katie had been through a number of boyfriends too, some of them looking serious for a while. A couple of times Jenna had comforted her friend while she wept for the ending of another relationship.

She'd thought herself lucky, secure in her certainty of Dean's steadfast love.

Now she knew better.

"If you and I were sleeping together," she said, "your family would know. We couldn't keep it a secret from them."

"So? They like you. Katie would be thrilled to bits."

"And what about when it ends?" Suppose they rejected her, out of family solidarity or embarrassment, or because it would be socially awkward to include their son's ex-lover? Especially if he'd acquired a new one. The ramifications could be endless. And heartbreaking. At the mere possibility of being shut out of their lives, all the fears and dreads of her childhood insecurities returned to haunt her.

If the Crossans rejected her, she'd be alone in the world. Even the thought of it made her shiver inwardly. She could feel again the intense, frightened loneliness she'd experienced at six years old, when she'd realized she could rely on no one but herself.

"I've no intention of letting it end," Marcus said.

"All your other affairs have. There'd be too many complications. I couldn't bear to lose my relationship with your family, Marcus." And if Marcus walked out of her life... Her heart quailed. "Or your friendship."

He took her hands in his. "You'll never lose that,

Jenna. It's yours for keeps. And I'm sure you won't lose Katie's, either...or Dean's. If that's what's bothering you, there's a very simple solution.''

Jenna shook her head. She couldn't see it. "It's too risky..."

"Listen," he urged. "I want much more than a few months of sharing your bed. And I know you need more than that. It wasn't Dean you wanted so much as what he symbolized for you—family, permanence and security, and those I'm more than happy to offer you. Marry me.''

At first Jenna thought she hadn't heard correctly. She'd been about to argue with his assessment of her love for Dean, but his final words drove everything else out of her head. She froze, showing no reaction at all.

Marcus was studying her intently. "Well?" he said, when the silence had stretched to almost five seconds. "Will you marry me, Jenna?"

Somehow she unglued her tongue from the roof of her mouth. "You don't want to get married! I mean...you've never shown any inclination to—''

For a split second he looked as though he might argue. Then he said, "Don't you think it's time I did? Most of my friends are married or with partners.''

"I thought you were quite happy.''

"Did you?" His voice flattened. "Well, perhaps there's been something missing from my life that you didn't know about.''

A wife? She looked at him and realized that although she'd known him for so long, there had always been something about Marcus that was hidden from her. She'd put it down to his being older, but the gap wasn't really so huge now. Yet he'd still seemed a little aloof. She knew him less well than she did any other member of his family.

And now he was proposing the most intimate relationship of all between man and woman.

His glance slipped over her, a crooked smile on his mouth. "I want you very much, Jenna, and I would love you...to be my wife."

Assuaging a sexual urge, however powerful, didn't seem sufficient reason to make such a binding commitment. "If you're doing this to get me into bed—" she started, before his look stopped her, sending a tremor of trepidation through her.

"You know," his voice was deceptively gentle, "I find that somewhat offensive."

"I'm sorry." She knew he wasn't that crude—or that desperate. He genuinely liked her, and maybe that was enough for him. Not for her. "I can't marry a man I don't love!"

He regarded her narrowly for a moment, and shoved his hands into his pockets. His tone became crisp, almost businesslike. "You love my parents, don't you?"

"Yes, but that's diff—"

"What about Jane?"

"I'm very fond of her."

"And Katie."

"Of course!"

He paused. "And you dote on Dean. Are you saying I'm the only member of my family you don't love?"

"You know it's not the same!"

"So you do love me."

"In a way, of course—"

"A way that includes sex—lust—whatever you want to call it. An adult emotion, Jenna, not a rosy adolescent illusion. And I love you…" Again he paused. "I'd say we have a pretty sound basis for marriage."

"It's crazy," she said. Her head spun, and pulses throbbed at her temple and throat.

"Why? Every day people who were perfect strangers months—even weeks or days ago—promise to love and cherish each other until death. We've known each other nearly all your life. No nasty surprises, and certainly no hostile in-laws."

His reasoning was cogent. She didn't expect to love again as she'd loved Dean. Marcus aroused sexual feelings she hadn't even known she was capable of. And they had lots of things in common.

He had put his finger on the most persuasive argument of all—the promise of cementing her place in his family, strengthening the bonds that were so important to her.

"Children," she said. Was she really seriously considering this? "Do you want children?" If there were children there would be no question of divorce. She'd never do that to a child. And she was sure Marcus wouldn't, either.

"I hope we'll have them," he said. "You like kids, don't you?"

She had always assumed one day she'd have a family. But not without benefit of wedlock. She wanted her children to have a father, one who was committed to them for life.

Everything he said made sense, and yet…

He reached for her, drawing her closer, his hands gliding up her arms and over her shoulders to hold her head. His lips met hers in a long, tender, drugging kiss, utterly different from the heart-pounding rage of passion earlier. "We have more than sex," he told her. "Though that's important, and I want it, with you. If you hadn't shown me you want it too, I wouldn't have forced the issue. Oh, I know," he said as she opened her lips to speak. "Your heart belongs to Dean. I can live with that until you get over it. One day you'll find you have your heart back—a bit bruised perhaps, but yours again. Because he doesn't want it."

She wasn't sure which came first, the hard pressure of his lips on hers or the sound of Katie's key in the lock.

If he heard it Marcus took no notice, nor of her hands pushing at his shoulders. He was intent on prying her lips apart, exploring her mouth with his.

Katie's voice said, "That's Marcus's car outside," and then, closer, "Are you two still...ooh, sorry! Are we interrupting something?"

She was standing in the doorway of the living room, with Jason behind her. Marcus at last loosened his grip on Jenna, though he still had his arm about her as he turned to his sister.

"You are," he said calmly.

"We could go out and come in again?" Katie offered, her eyes avid, an intrigued, pleased smile on her mouth.

"No," Jenna said. "I'll walk Marcus to the door."

"You're leaving?" Katie looked up at her brother.

"It seems so." He followed Jenna as she escaped his light hold and passed the other two.

Jenna opened the door for him, and a couple of small moths fluttered into the hallway. Marcus stopped, looking down into her upturned face.

He was right, she thought. Dean didn't want her, but Marcus, for whatever reason, apparently did. And her stupid, disillusioned heart would mend one day.

He lifted one hand and grasped the door behind her. It seemed neither of them knew what to do next.

"Think about it," he said, and bent his head to hers, but the kiss was so quick she hardly had time to respond. "I'll call you tomorrow."

He kissed her again, this time more lingeringly. Then he left her, and she waited until he'd driven off before she closed the door, and discovered that her knees were shaking.

After leaning on the door for a few seconds, she made her way back into the living room. "I'm going to bed," she announced, pretending not to notice the enthralled interest on Katie's face.

It was barely fifteen minutes before she heard Jason depart, and seconds later Katie opened Jenna's bedroom door.

"You can't be asleep yet," she declared.

Jenna sighed and struggled up, switching the bedside light on.

Katie grinned at her and sprawled across the end of the bed. "Come on, what's going on between you and big brother?"

"He asked me to marry him."

Katie's mouth opened on a strangled squeak. "He

did? I can't *believe* it!'' She flung herself across the bed to hug her friend.

''I hardly believe it myself,'' Jenna muttered.

''You'll be my sister-in-law!'' Katie said excitedly. ''Well, I always thought you would be, but that was when—'' She broke off and hugged Jenna again. ''I told you he fancied you! You said yes, didn't you?''

''No, not yet.'' She mustn't let Katie's enthusiasm influence her decision.

''Why not?'' Katie clapped a hand over her mouth, her eyes rounding. ''Oh, sorry. We interrupted, didn't we! The air was positively sizzling tonight when we walked in.''

''It's all right. Probably just as well. It gives me time to think.''

''About what? I know you, Jen. You wouldn't kiss a guy that way unless you meant it. When did you realize you were in love?''

She couldn't tell Katie they weren't in love, really. ''I suppose tonight,'' she said reluctantly.

''The family's going to be so rapt!'' Katie said. ''You'll be legally one of us. Can we tell Mum and Dad tomorrow? Or does Marcus want to do it?''

''I haven't said yes,'' Jenna reminded her.

''Of course you're going to say yes! You and Marcus—it's perfect! I don't know why none of us realized before. You're both a bit reserved and serious, deep waters and all that, and you like heaps of the same things! He's always looked out for you, but you were the one who stood up to him when we were kids. He needs someone he can't push around. You're obviously made for each other.''

''We are?''

"Totally. But I guess you know that. Wait till I tell Dean!"

"You can't!"

"Well, not until you've said yes, I suppose," Katie sulked. She gave a little bounce on the bed, sitting up. "Phone him."

"Phone Dean?"

"Marcus, you idiot! Phone him and put the poor man out of his misery. He'll be home by now."

She bounded into the sitting room and came back with the portable receiver in her hand, thrusting it at Jenna before sitting cross-legged on the bed.

Her delighted enthusiasm was hard to resist. Apparently it didn't occur to her to give Jenna privacy. "Go on," she urged, and reeled off the number.

Why not? Jenna thought recklessly. Of course she wasn't doing it simply because she didn't want to disappoint Katie. There were lots of other, better reasons. If all the Crossans felt as Katie did, and Dean was going to marry Callie anyway, why shouldn't she accept Marcus's proposal? It was probably the best offer she'd get.

Nearly perfect, in fact, except that he was the wrong man. Which he knew and didn't seem to mind. It wasn't as though she would be doing it under false pretences. He himself had used the incentive of a closer tie to his family, knowing what a tempting bait that was for her.

As if in a dream her fingers pressed the buttons. She lifted the receiver to her ear and heard the ringing tone. Maybe he wasn't home yet after all.

Then his voice said, strong and deep in her ear, "Hello?"

"Marcus?" Her hand was shaking and damp. She licked her lips.

"Jenna." He waited.

She looked up at Katie who nodded vigorously, both thumbs held up, a huge, encouraging smile on her face.

Jenna cleared her throat. "I just want to say…the answer's yes."

For a minute she was afraid he hadn't heard. Then she heard him let out a breath. "Thank you," he said. "Thank you very much, darling."

Darling. Strangely, her heart seemed to melt, turning to a warm little mass. "Thank *you*," she whispered, "for asking me."

He laughed rather unsteadily. "That's very sweet. I thought you'd be in bed by now."

"I'm calling from there."

He made a soft, indefinable sound. "I'll let you sleep then. And Jenna…?"

"Yes?"

"I love you. I'm glad you called."

"I…I love you too," she said, conscious of Katie shamelessly listening. It wasn't a lie. As he'd pointed out, there were different kinds of love.

Marcus bought her a solitaire diamond set in a narrow hoop of gold. Later she phoned her mother with the news while he sat at her side.

"She's pleased," she said, handing him the receiver. "She wants to talk to you."

He took Jenna's hand in his free one, playing with the new ring on her finger while he spoke to her mother. "Yes," he said. "Thank you. And I'm a lucky man.... We haven't discussed the date, but very soon.''

Jenna looked up at him, her eyes widening, and he went on talking to Karen. ''I thought we'd have it here in Auckland, if you don't object. Of course we'll consult you about arrangements. My mother will be delighted to help.... Sure...here she is again.'' He handed the receiver back to Jenna.

After she'd hung up he said, ''Do you want a big affair with all the trimmings?''

''No!''

''Sure?'' His look was penetrating.

''Absolutely.''

''That's good, because I'd like to do this quietly. And quickly.''

''Quickly?'' Her heart skipped a beat.

''I don't see any reason to wait, do you?''

Jenna swallowed. ''I suppose not.''

''Are you having second thoughts?'' He looked grim, his hand tightening fractionally on hers.

''Are *you*?'' she asked him.

''No. I know what I want, Jenna.''

Jenna sat in silence for a second or two. For so long a time she had wanted Dean. It was difficult to break the habit. But she must move on—*had* moved on.

She'd agreed to marry Marcus, who wanted her in a way that Dean never had.

And she wanted him in the most fundamental, physical way, at least. He was an attractive, sexy man with his own successful business, and she knew he was decent, hardworking, kind. What more could any woman ask for?

She lifted her head. "I said I'd marry you. I won't go back on it."

"Good." She saw him relax. "Will a month give you enough time to get a dress and do whatever else you need to?"

"A month?" Her eyes widened.

"Why not?"

"Dean…" she said feebly "…and Callie."

Marcus's face had gone taut and narrow-eyed. "What about them?"

"We shouldn't steal their thunder. I mean, getting married before them. They were engaged first."

Katie had suggested a double wedding, to Jenna's dismay. Marcus had retorted curtly he had no intention of sharing his wedding day with anyone except his bride.

His eyes held hers, seeming to search the depths. "They haven't set a date," he said. "And I don't feel inclined to hold back until they do."

He held back in other ways during the next four weeks. Jenna had capitulated on the date after Katie told her that Callie and her parents were still discussing whether the wedding would be in America or New Zealand. "Her parents would like to give her a traditional wedding over there, and naturally Callie wants her friends around her. Mum and Dad are happy to have it here, but either way one family's going to have to travel."

Compared with the logistics of that wedding, Jenna and Marcus's was an exercise in simplicity. Katie helped Jenna choose an off-the-peg white silk dress trimmed with teardrop pearls. Marcus booked a chapel close to his parents' home, and the guest list was limited to the families and about twenty friends.

Marcus hired caterers, vetoing his mother's offer of doing the food herself. "I said a small celebration," he told her, "not a cheap one. And I want you to enjoy yourself, not be worrying over heating savories and whipping cream."

Katie was Jenna's only attendant, and Dean waited beside his brother at the altar. There was no way Marcus could have asked anyone else.

Escorted down the aisle by her stepfather, Jenna kept her gaze straight ahead.

When she raised her eyes to his face, Marcus looked serious and tense, but his lips moved in a slight smile as the celebrant began the marriage service.

Jenna spoke her responses in a voice that shook only slightly. Marcus made his firmly, but when he placed the ring on her finger she noticed his were trembling, so that he fumbled a little before slipping it over her knuckle.

He lifted back the short veil and kissed her, his lips warm and somehow reassuring. His hand was firmly wound about hers as they went to sign the register, and when they walked back along the length of the chapel.

Dean slapped his brother's back and kissed Jenna briefly on the lips. She hardly felt it. Katie hugged her exuberantly, and her mother, smiling mistily, came to kiss her cheek, followed by Mrs. Crossan.

There were photographs and congratulations and, back at the Crossans' house, a babble of noise, lots of champagne, more congratulations and a few short speeches.

She was aware of Marcus at her side, taking her arm, seeing that she had a drink, making her eat something. But everything was a blur until they left the house and ran to his car.

They hadn't escaped a hail of confetti. Jenna flicked it from her sleeves and shook out her skirt, and once he was sure they hadn't been followed, Marcus stopped the car and brushed some from his shoulders, then ruffled his fingers through his hair, scattering tiny rounds on the floor of the car.

"There's more," Jenna told him.

"You do it." He bent his head for her, and she reached up to pick out the stray scraps of color. His hair was soft and warm against her fingers.

"Thanks," he said when she sat back. "My turn."

She felt the light touch of his fingers in her hair, moving through it. When he was done he smoothed it back over one ear and his hand curved about her nape while a thumb stroked her cheek. "All right?" he asked quietly.

"Yes."

He studied her face. "Not nervous of me, are you, Jenna?"

Jenna bit her lip. She felt tense, and foolish. "Not of you."

"Of this whole business?" he guessed. His thumb moved over her mouth, and a pleasurable sensation uncurled in her midriff.

Marcus said, "I won't hurry you. We're married. There's a whole lifetime ahead of us."

He leaned forward and gave her a quick, reassuring kiss. Then he released her and restarted the car.

Chapter Eight

During their short engagement Marcus's kisses had been passionate, his caresses sometimes intimate. But he had stopped their lovemaking short of consummation, leaving Jenna tense and dissatisfied.

She supposed he was respecting her virginity, and she had always intended to be a virgin bride, but she sometimes wondered if he was deliberately keeping her in a state of suspense so she wouldn't want to delay the wedding. The breathtaking speed with which he'd arranged everything indicated that he might not be sure she'd go through with it.

Well, she had. And now, as he'd said, they were married, with a lifetime ahead of them.

But first there was tonight.

Marcus had booked them into a city hotel where they would stay before flying to Rarotonga in the Cook Islands for a week.

The room wasn't the honeymoon suite, but it had

a magnificent view of the blue-green expanse of the
Waitemata Harbor—and sported a king-size bed. A
small table flanked by easy chairs held a foil-topped
bottle and two glass flutes.

Jenna averted her eyes from the bed and went to
the windows. Dusk was falling. Lights flickered on
along the water's edge and outlined the ships tied up
at the wharf, reflected in wavy lines that appeared to
plunge into the restless sea.

Marcus came to stand beside her, an arm about her
shoulders, and they watched in silence as more lights
winked on and the water darkened. A few pale stars
jeweled the sky.

He moved his hand to the back of her neck and
began massaging it. It was soothing and yet erotic.
She tipped her head forward, allowing his clever,
strong fingers to ease away the tension that had held
her all day.

"I thought we might ask room service to send up
a meal," he said.

"Mmm. All right." When his fingers stilled on her
nape, she tipped her head back against his hand.

He dipped his head swiftly, his lips meeting hers
as he stepped close and angled her to him.

Jenna answered his kiss without pretense, her lips
parted and eager, and after a few moments she turned
to him, her arms sliding around his shoulders. He
went momentarily still as if taken aback, then his fingers were in her hair and the kiss became deeper, their
bodies pressing close.

Marcus lifted his head, and his hands skimmed
down her back, closed about her hips to put an inch
or two of space between them. His eyes were very

dark, and a layer of color outlined his cheekbones. "About that meal," he said, his voice low and rasping.

"What meal?" Jenna's arms were still loosely hooked about his neck, and she sent him a calculatedly provocative look.

Marcus appeared slightly dazed. "The one I thought we'd have with the champagne." He indicated the bottle on the table. "Before..."

"Do you plan to get me drunk again?"

His mouth curved in a bemused smile. "A bit more relaxed. I thought you were scared."

A tremor of nervous excitement fluttered in her stomach. "There has to be a first time."

The smile became strained. "It doesn't have to be tonight," he said gravely. "Not if you'd rather wait."

Something melted warmly inside her. Despite his haste to marry her, and the desire he hadn't tried to hide, he was still prepared to let her set the pace. That was a gesture of chivalry she hadn't expected, and yet it was characteristic of Marcus.

She touched her tongue to her lips. "I don't want to wait. Do you?"

His chest moved on a harsh breath. He tightened his hands again on her hips and brought her close to him. "In the stupid-questions department, my darling wife," he said, "that takes first prize."

She was laughing when he kissed her again, stifling the laughter with his mouth, and she wound her arms about him and clung while she kissed him back without inhibition, teasing him with her tongue and her teeth.

He drew away, breathing hard, and looked down at

her with narrow, glittering eyes. "Who taught you to kiss like that?"

"You did," she taunted breathlessly. "Are you complaining?"

"Hell, no!" Without warning he picked her up in his arms and strode to the bed, lowering her onto the cover.

She kicked her shoes to the floor. Marcus sat on the bed and bent to remove his shoes and socks, threw off his jacket and unbuttoned his shirt, discarding that too.

Jenna watched, her heart beating fast and hard, a delicious desire suffusing her body.

Marcus stood up and went back to the table, dispensed with the foil top and the cork on the bottle, and poured champagne into the flutes as vapor curled from the neck.

He carried the glasses and bottle to the night table by the bed and put them down. "Move over."

When she had, he turned back the bed covers and stacked a couple of pillows, inviting her to lean on them while he dealt with the other half of the bed.

He settled beside her and handed her a glass, clicked his against it. "To us."

Holding her eyes with his, he half emptied his glass. Jenna sipped at hers, the crisp, tart bubbles bursting on her tongue.

And then Marcus closed the few inches between them, and she felt his tongue on her lips, tasting the champagne.

She made a small, startled sound, and he drew back. "You don't like it?" He looked at her questioningly.

"No! I mean, it's not that."

He smiled slowly. "You do like it?"

She had to swallow some more of the champagne before answering. "Yes."

"Good," he said. "Tell me if I do anything you don't like." And he lowered his head again.

He dipped a forefinger into his glass and touched it to the hollow at the base of her throat, and she felt the coolness before he bent forward again and licked the wine away.

Jenna's lips parted and a wild heat flared in her cheeks. His eyes gleaming slits, Marcus kissed her again, deep and demanding, pressing her back against the pillows. The glass she held shook so much that some of the liquid spilled over her hand.

When they surfaced from the kiss he looked the way she felt—dazed and aroused. A trickle of champagne moistened his shoulder, and a lone droplet ran down to his chest. Daringly, she leaned forward and captured it with her tongue.

Marcus sucked in an audible breath. He downed the remainder of his drink in a single swallow and placed the glass on the night table. With an air of determination he began to undo the buttons on the front of her shirt.

The lace cups of her bra barely covered half her breasts, leaving the rest exposed to his gaze. Her heart thumped as he looked his fill before tracing the outline of the lace with a fingertip. He pushed the shirt from her shoulders and she helped him get it off.

Then he snapped open the fastener of her pants, and unzipped them.

"Lift up," he said, and she helped him peel off the pants.

Underneath she wore a minuscule garment that matched her bra.

"Very nice."

Jenna gulped down some more of her wine. She was both nervous and fascinated.

Then he leaned over and kissed her again.

A sweet tension began to build inside her. Her head buzzed. She tightened her fingers on the glass in her hand and made a frantic little movement.

Marcus withdrew his mouth from hers and took the glass, placing it beside his own, then he was shifting her farther down the bed, kissing her again, his hands making wonderful magic. And she reciprocated, finding his body unfamiliar but increasingly fascinating.

At last Jenna made an inarticulate sound in her throat. Marcus lifted his head. "Yes?"

"Yes." She could hardly get the single word out.

He smoothed her tumbled hair and kissed her forehead. "There's nothing to be frightened of."

Jenna wasn't frightened; she was desperate for him. And desperately grateful for his careful initiation.

It was both strange and exciting. When he glided home, the fragile barrier stopped him, and she saw his cheeks tauten. He stilled, waiting for her, breathing cautiously.

Jenna moved tentatively, then as the barrier frustrated her she set her teeth and took the initiative.

It hurt, and she cried out softly in pain.

"I'm sorry, darling," she heard Marcus say. "If you want to stop…"

Fiercely she shook her head, and closed her teeth on her lower lip.

The barrier was gone. The hurt lessened. And soon she was soaring, and knew that he too had reached the pinnacle, holding her tightly while they both shuddered into quiescence, panting against each other.

He turned to her and kissed her deeply. Then his lips left hers and he said, "Are you all right?"

"Perfectly." She hung her arms about his neck. "Are you?"

"Need you ask?" He kissed her again. "I knew you could be a wonderful lover, but I didn't expect it to be so fantastic the first time."

"Neither did I," she confessed. "Thank you, Marcus."

"Don't say that. Thank you for marrying me, Jenna. And for being so courageous and utterly beautiful. You were stunning."

Jenna was glad she had pleased him. She felt nicely floaty, and when he withdrew from her she experienced a sense of loss.

Later they showered and decorously sat down to a room service meal and more champagne.

And still later they were back in bed and in each other's arms.

That was how they spent most of the next week, between walking along white coral-sand beaches and snorkeling in sparkling clear water, dining on exotic coconut-flavored dishes and watching the Cook Island dancers who provided entertainment at their hotel.

The dancing was sensuous and flirtatious, the men half crouching and slapping their brown, muscular

thighs together as they circled the women, who se-
ductively swayed their hips, eyes demurely downcast,
while the wooden drums that accompanied them kept
up a clamorous rhythm.

Marcus hired a motor scooter, the chief form of
transport, and they circled the island, Jenna clinging
to him with her arms about his waist. He drove up
through coconut and taro plantations to the hilly interior, and they walked under tall yellow-flowered hibiscus trees and raggedy-leaved banana trees with
huge dark-wine velvet flowers and found a secluded
little glade where moss cushioned their bodies as they
made love sheltered by a circle of close-growing
trees.

"This is a slice of heaven," she breathed afterward, as she lay in Marcus's arms, watching the lat-
ticework of leaves overhead shift against the sun. Distantly she could hear the waves breaking on the reef
surrounding the island. Close by the palms shivered
and swayed. "It really is a tropical paradise."

"Paradise is where you make it," Marcus replied.
"But..." He looked down at her, smoothing a strand
of hair from her forehead. "I'll never forget this. I
want to make you happy, Jenna. And keep you happy
forever."

On their last night on the island, when the guests
were invited to join in the island dancing, Marcus
surprised Jenna by pulling her to her feet. Laughing
at her protest, he put his hands on her hips and challenged her to imitate the women dancers, while he
followed the men's example.

At first self-conscious, she soon picked up the

rhythm and began to enjoy herself. The drumbeat became faster and faster, a frenetic, dazzling display, and when it stopped she was breathless.

The dancers left to a storm of applause, and a three-piece band began to play a jazz tune. Instead of leading her back to their table, Marcus folded Jenna into his arms and moved to the music among other couples taking the floor.

Tonight Jenna had worn one of the hand-dyed cotton sarongs sold in the local markets, knotting it about her waist so that it fell to her ankles, teaming it with a white cropped top. Marcus's hands were on her skin, a thumb subtly tracing the groove of her spine.

His chin brushed her temple, and his thighs flexed against hers. The lights dimmed and she closed her eyes, enjoying the spell cast by the tropical night, the music, and the man holding her.

She felt alive and content—more so than she had in years. For a long time she'd been in a sort of suspended animation, waiting for her life to take up where it had left off.

And now it had taken a different direction. She had woken from a dream and found reality infinitely more exciting and satisfying.

Tightening her arms about Marcus's neck, she laid her cheek against his shoulder. When the music stopped he didn't let her go immediately, but murmured, "Shall we go now?"

"Yes." She wanted him. Wanted his hands on her body, his mouth on hers, wanted him inside her again, taking her to heights of pleasure that seemed to grow more intense every time they were together.

The hotel was all on one level, its guest quarters

individual thatch-roofed units secluded by tall, gracefully bowed palms, heavy-scented frangipani trees and glossy red-leaved shrubs. Low lights among the shrubbery lit the path back to their unit.

Inside, screened windows allowed the scent of the frangipani to perfume the bedroom, and through the lattice of palm leaves a full moon lit the wide bed, turning the sheets blue-white.

Jenna was admiring the moon framed by the big window when Marcus came up behind her and linked his fingers at her bare waist. He kissed her neck, and Jenna leaned back against him.

He turned her and backed her against the wall and kissed her until she was dizzy. When he began tugging at the knot of the pareu, Jenna reciprocated by undoing the buttons of his shirt. She pressed herself against him and felt with triumph the surge of his response.

Naked, they fell on the bed together, and within seconds her small cries of fulfillment were joined by his low groans of satisfaction.

In the aftermath she turned to him, his sweat-sheened body lit in restless bars of moonlight as the palm tree outside whispered harshly in the wind. His face was in shadow, but he wound his fingers into her hair and kissed her again.

Jenna rested her head against his shoulder and felt him let out a long breath. Her skin tingled, and her limbs were twined with his. She turned her head to kiss his salty skin, and his hold on her tightened. She felt remarkably content, happier than she could ever remember. She had never been so close to another human being.

* * *

It was a night she was to remember for a long time. Something magical and intimate that they shared before returning to New Zealand and a different kind of reality.

Reality now was going back to work and spending the days apart from Marcus. But it was also settling herself into his apartment and into his lifestyle.

He made room for her clothes in his bedroom. She found space for her toiletries and makeup in the bathroom, and filled his kitchen cupboards with condiments, spices and ingredients that he'd never bought himself.

"I generally eat out or order something in," he told her the first time he came home to find her preparing a meal. "You're working too. There's no need to rush home and make dinner for me."

"I like cooking." Jenna opened the oven to insert a tray of duchesse potatoes. "If you don't want me to—"

"I didn't say that. Only it wasn't my intention to turn you into a housewife."

"You're not turning me into anything," Jenna said firmly. "Pass me that glass bowl over there, will you? I need it for the salad."

He passed it, and left to change out of his business suit into casual slacks and a T-shirt.

Over the filet mignon and fresh vegetables she'd prepared, he said, "This is great. I'm not much of a cook myself."

Jenna looked at him curiously. "You made me breakfast when I stayed here, the night the flat was flooded."

''Ah, breakfast is different. On weekends I often do bacon and eggs.''

For two? Unreasonably, Jenna was pierced with jealousy, wondering how many women had sat at this table after a night of passion—how many had shared his bed.

Don't be silly, she admonished herself. He didn't marry any of them, did he?

He had married her—Jenna. Because he was ready to settle down, and preferred to do so with someone he'd known for years.

It sounded sensible—and boring.

''Do you like being married?'' she asked him.

''I like being married to you, Jenna.'' He paused. ''Do you like it?''

''Yes.'' She liked being with him and certainly was never bored. Besides having a quiet sense of humor and a kind heart, Marcus was an inventive, exciting lover. Jenna knew she had surprised and delighted him by matching his appetite, if not his expertise. They challenged each other to new heights of pleasure, often until they were both exhausted. And he was always careful of her pleasure as well as his own.

She glanced away from the rather penetrating look he was giving her. ''You're a very considerate husband, Marcus.''

He stood up abruptly and started clearing away plates. ''I guess that's my cue.''

Jenna hadn't realized what a full social life Marcus had. There were dinner parties and weekend yachting parties, and business occasions when Marcus asked her to accompany him.

His friends seemed happy to welcome Marcus's wife. His business partner's wife in particular was warm in her congratulations. As she and Jenna renewed their lipstick in the ladies' room after a restaurant meal with potential clients, she said, "Marcus has been wrapped up in the business far too long. It's time he had a real relationship."

"He's had girlfriends," Jenna ventured.

"Hmm." Angela Travers tossed her dark curls, her normally soft, pretty mouth thinning. "None of them were what he needs." She took a tissue from a box on the counter and blotted her lipstick.

"What do you think he needs?" Jenna asked.

"Someone who puts him first," Angela said frankly. "Who truly loves him and isn't just using him, who won't let him down."

Feeling a pang of guilt, Jenna said, "Has he been let down?"

Angela hesitated. "I don't know for sure. I've always had a feeling that he's hurting deep inside. And that none of those women he's been with have helped much. You've known him forever, haven't you? I thought you'd know."

Jenna shook her head. "He's older, and when we were kids the gap seemed huge. Since he left home I've only seen him at family gatherings, really. Until recently, that is," she added hastily.

"But you do love him?"

"I've always loved him." It was true, although of course it was different from the way she'd felt for Dean.

Different, but...? All that angst over Dean now paled into a fuzzy memory. Teenage romanticism,

Marcus had scathingly called it. Puppy love. Could he have been right?

Apologetically the other woman said, ''I have no business cross-questioning you. It's just that Ted and I are very fond of Marcus, and we want him to be happy.''

''So do I.'' She owed him that.

''Of course you do.'' Angela squeezed her arm. ''I shouldn't be butting in. Put it down to the wine. I've never had a good head for alcohol.''

Chapter Nine

They were invited to have dinner with Dean and Callie.

"How do you feel about that?" Marcus asked, studying her face.

Jenna shrugged. "We can't say no, can we?"

He didn't answer for a second. "I suppose not," he said finally. "We'd better accept, then."

Katie and Jason had been invited too, and the twins kept the conversation lively, each capping the other's jokes with some quick-witted reply. Callie smiled a lot, although she was quieter than usual.

Watching Dean as he laughed at something his sister had said, Jenna smiled too. She loved them both, and that would never change, but with a sense of relief she realized that her feelings for Dean had radically altered. Affection was there, but there was no tearing heartache and no longing for a closer tie.

It was over. Dean was someone she was close to

but not intimate with. And compared with his older brother he seemed very young.

A new sensation of lightness and freedom washed over her. She was happy, almost wildly so. When Dean made some silly pun and Katie groaned loudly, Jenna capped it with one of her own, her eyes dancing, and the three of them were soon off into a teasing, laughing round of quip and counter-quip that had Callie giggling, Jason grinning in a slightly bewildered way, and Marcus's eyes moving from one to the other of them while his mouth curved and his cheek creased in amusement.

Dean poured more wine, and Callie said, ''It's great that you all get on so well together.''

''We've been friends forever,'' Dean said. ''I'm glad Marcus had the sense to marry Jenna. The best thing he ever did.''

''I concur with that,'' Marcus said lazily.

''Thank you, Dean,'' Jenna said graciously. ''I'm glad too.''

They grinned at each other, and the bubble of happiness inside her seemed to swell and burst in a rush of affection for him, unmixed with any sexual feelings at all. He was her old playmate again, and she was glad to have him back. Laughing from sheer exuberant relief, she turned to Marcus, and saw his eyes narrow. The laughter died and she gave him a radiant smile. How foolish she had been to imagine that her puppy love was the real thing. Now she knew what a pale imitation it had been of grown-up, lasting love. She couldn't imagine being married to anyone but Marcus.

When Callie got up to clear the plates and bring

the next course, Jenna followed her into the kitchen, offering help.

"You could cut that into wedges." Callie indicated the cheesecake on the table. "I'll just put some fruit salad in a bowl."

"This looks good." Jenna found a knife and began slicing.

"I bought it," Callie said, seeming embarrassed. "I'm not much of a cook." She took a can of fruit salad from a cupboard.

"The chicken was delicious," Jenna assured her.

Callie wrinkled her nose. "The rice went gluey."

"It was fine. No one complained, did they?"

"You're all too polite." Callie wrestled with the can opener. "Oh, heck—I can't even open a can!" Frustratedly she banged it on the counter.

"Let me help." Jenna abandoned the cheesecake and picked up the opener, making sure it was firmly seated before turning the wings. The wheel cut into the metal and soon she was removing the top.

"Thanks." Callie took the can and emptied it into a bowl. "At home we had an electric opener." She sniffed.

"You can buy them here." Jenna looked at the other girl's downbent head. "Are you all right, Callie?"

Callie sniffed again and dashed a hand across her eyes, but it didn't stop the tears Jenna saw spilling onto her cheeks.

She put an arm about Callie's shoulders. "Callie?"

"I'm all right." Callie grabbed a paper towel from the wall dispenser and dabbed her eyes and nose. "I *love* Dean,'' she said fiercely. ''Only sometimes I miss home. You won't tell him about this, will you?''

''Does he know how you feel?''

''He knows how I feel about him.''

''If you miss your home so much, shouldn't you tell him?''

''I don't want him to know what a baby I am.'' Callie squared her shoulders. ''If I carry this, can you bring in the cheesecake?''

''We should have Dean and Callie round to our place soon,'' Jenna said later as Marcus drove the car into the garage.

He pulled on the hand brake and switched off the lights. ''You wouldn't mind?''

''She needs friends.''

''I would have thought you'd be the last person on earth…''

''You want your brother to be happy, don't you?''

''Of course,'' he replied shortly. Pulling the key from the ignition, he got out of the car.

Inside, Jenna prepared herself for bed, pleasantly filled with food and wine and the memory of an enjoyable evening, except for Callie's sudden revelation of her homesickness.

Marcus hadn't come into the bedroom, and as she was about to climb between the sheets, she wondered what he was doing and returned to the living area to find out.

There were no lights on, but in the darkened living room he stood, a dark, shadowy figure at the window, looking out at the lights of the city.

''Marcus?''

He turned at the sound of her voice, and she saw the faint gleam of a glass in his hand.

She went to join him, the satin of her nightgown sliding against her thighs as she approached. "What are you doing?"

"Having a nightcap," he answered, adding after a second, "Do you want one?" He sounded remote and polite and she couldn't see his face.

"No, I've had enough alcohol tonight." He had drunk very little, pacing himself because he was driving. Marcus had never been a heavy drinker.

She stood at his side, watching the winking lights, while he tossed off the remainder of the drink and put down the glass on the sill. A spatter of rain hit the window, and ran crookedly down the pane, picking up diamond points of lights on the way. Jenna felt goose bumps on her flesh and crossed her arms in front of her.

"You're cold." Marcus put an arm about her, rubbing his slightly roughened palm over her suddenly cooled skin.

"Not really."

The rain outside intensified, blurring the view, all the lights running together like an abstract painting. She looked up and saw Marcus's face in profile, jutting against the window, strong and impenetrable. She did feel cold, then. Cold and shut out.

"Marcus?" She said his name again, and he turned slowly, as if he'd just remembered she was there.

"What is it, Jenna?" he asked gently.

He must have heard the troubled note in her voice. "Nothing," she said. "Are you coming to bed?"

"Are you inviting me?"

Her heart quickened. "Do you need an invitation?" She paused. "You know you're always welcome."

"Always?"

She had never refused him unless for obvious reasons. "Of course. Surely you know that?"

"Men don't always know for sure. Women can pretend."

She'd never have thought Marcus was lacking in confidence. She tried to see his face, but it was too dark to discern his expression. "I don't pretend," she said. "I wouldn't. And besides, there's no need."

"You don't...fantasize?"

The only fantasizing she did was when he wasn't around and she was thinking about him. "Do you?" she asked point-blank. Did he see some film star or pin-up in his mind when he was making love to her?

"Why would I want to?" he said, turning to bring her into the circle of his arms. "When the embodiment of all my fantasies is right here?"

An extravagant thing to say, that would please any woman. She didn't know why it caused her a slight pang. Perhaps because she couldn't quite believe it. To banish the small doubt, she lifted her face to him in invitation and slid her arms around his neck. "Thank you, Marcus."

Their lips met in a long, increasingly passionate kiss. Through the thin satin gown she felt the heat and hardness of his body as he crushed her closer, and their breathing quickened. They didn't even get as far as the bedroom before he had discarded his clothing and pulled off her nightgown. The sofa was wide and soft and Marcus arranged the cushions for her comfort. In the darkness, with the rain beating on the windows, they came together, and Marcus muttered hoarsely, urgently, "Say my name, Jenna. Tell me you know who I am."

Almost lost in sensation, too caught up in the whirlwind to wonder why he needed this, she gasped it out, and heard him groan aloud when they reached at last a mutual fulfillment.

As they lay panting in each other's arms for minutes afterward, Jenna asked him, "Did that feel like pretending?"

She felt the heave of his breath, followed by silent laughter. "No," he said before he picked her up in his arms and carried her to their bed. "It felt like...nothing else on earth."

It wasn't the first or the last time they had not bothered with a bed. They had made love on the couch, on the floor, once in an armchair, even in the kitchen and bathroom, and a few times in the car when they'd been too impatient to wait until they were home after a night out.

Sometimes it seemed to Jenna there was a kind of desperation to their lovemaking that gave her an uneasy feeling. It was almost as if it was their only sure avenue of communication.

They had agreed that there was no need to prevent pregnancy. But despite their very active sex life, four months into their marriage Jenna's cycle was as regular as ever.

Marcus's mother chuckled when Jenna mentioned the fact. "Not everyone gets pregnant at the drop of a hat, you know. If you go more than a year or so it might be wise to get a doctor to check you out. Meantime the best thing you can do is relax. I'm sure Marcus doesn't mind.''

But there were odd occasions when she caught him watching her as if waiting for something. Maybe he felt more strongly about having children than he was letting on.

Then Katie phoned her at work one day, sounding agitated. ''It's Dean,'' she blurted, and Jenna's heart stopped for an instant. ''Callie's left.''

''Left?'' Jenna was dazed. Callie had left Dean?

''He's devastated,'' Katie told her. ''He's a mess.''

''Where is he? And where's Callie gone?''

''Home. Callie, I mean. Back to America. Dean spent the night at the flat with me. I'm worried about him, Jenna. Can you help?''

''What do you want me to do?''

''Jason and I are having dinner at his parents' place tonight. It's all arranged and I don't want to let him down, but I hate the thought of Dean going home to that empty house after work.''

''Don't worry, Katie,'' Jenna said immediately. ''I'll see he isn't alone.''

She was waiting outside his place when Dean turned up. He looked at her dully, without surprise. ''Katie told you,'' he said.

''Yes.'' Jenna touched his arm. ''I'm so sorry.''

He opened the door, taking it for granted she'd come in. He looked worn and pale, his mouth set in a stubborn line. ''It's nice of you to come, but I don't need a nursemaid.''

''I'm not a nursemaid, I'm a friend. And your sister-in-law. Next best thing to a sister.''

He managed a wan smile. "Can I make you a drink? I'm heading for the whiskey myself."

Jenna forbore to ask him if that was wise. If he wanted to drown his sorrows, she guessed he was entitled.

"Gin and lemon?" he asked her, and she nodded.

She sat on the sofa while Dean paced the sitting room, glancing out the window to the street, picking up books and ornaments and putting them down again as if he didn't know what to do with himself between gulping at his drink.

"Do you want to talk about it?" she asked quietly.

A photograph of Callie, laughing into the camera, stood on top of a bookcase. Dean picked it up and stared down at it. "Am I an insensitive sod, Jenna? Should I have noticed she was unhappy?"

"She wasn't unhappy all the time."

He brightened a bit. "She wasn't, was she? I mean, she can't have been pretending every time we..." Then he looked grim again. "But it was a tug-of-war between me and her old life. And I lost."

"Did you fight over it?"

He shook his head. "No. We cried over it." He looked embarrassed and buried his nose in the whiskey glass. "I took her to the airport," he said, lowering the glass and staring moodily into it. "Still hoping she'd change her mind."

When Jenna returned to the apartment, Marcus was on the sofa, a stack of papers on the coffee table before him, a pen in his hand and an empty shot glass at his elbow. He wore his business shirt but had unbuttoned the collar and rolled up the sleeves.

His gaze was alert and questioning. "You look whacked," he said. "Do you need a drink?"

"I've had enough to drink, thanks."

Marcus's brows went up. "Is that so?"

Not as much as Dean, whom she'd left curled up on the sofa where he'd finally collapsed. She'd removed his shoes and thrown a light blanket over him before leaving.

"A couple of glasses of gin and lemon," she explained, "with Dean. You got my message?" She'd left a message on the answering machine to say where she was, but with Dean listening in she hadn't gone into detail about why.

"How is Dean—and Callie? Is something wrong?"

"She's gone," Jenna told him. "Back to America."

His stillness was almost frightening. He might have been turned to stone, not even blinking as his darkened eyes bored into hers. "She's left him?"

"She was homesick. More than Dean ever realized, I think. He's terribly upset, and Katie was meeting Jason's parents tonight."

Marcus was scrutinizing her face. "So you went to comfort him."

"He needed someone." Jenna's eyes filled with tears. She was tired and wrung out after being supportive and sympathetic for hours while Dean talked and cried and finally drank himself into temporary oblivion. His shock and bewilderment and self-blame had made her own heart ache.

She wiped at the tears with her hand. Marcus didn't move, so she said, "I'm going to bed."

In the bathroom she splashed cold water on her

eyes and blew her nose. Poor Dean. And poor Callie. She felt wretchedly sorry for them both.

She was in the bedroom when the sound of breaking glass made her start. Marcus must have dropped something. She put on a silky nightgown and got into bed. She desperately wanted Marcus beside her, his warm, hard body close to hers. She wanted to make love to him, to feel his mouth on her lips and her body, his thighs strong and muscular between her own.

But by the time he slid into the bed beside her she had long been claimed by sleep.

In the morning she was lethargic and depressed. Marcus too seemed almost morose.

There was something wrapped in newspaper on the counter, and when Jenna picked it up Marcus said quickly, "Careful—I should have put that in the bin."

She looked at him.

"I...dropped a glass last night," he explained.

Dimly she recalled hearing the crash.

Marcus was putting folders into his briefcase when the phone rang and he handed the receiver to Jenna.

"How was he?" Katie asked.

"Sleeping like a baby when I left," Jenna reported. "Pretty cut up, actually. He'd had a lot of whiskey."

Marcus stopped by her and gave her a cool kiss on her cheek. He spoke into the receiver. "Jenna has to go to work, Katie. Why don't you phone Dean?"

"I have, and he's not answering," Katie said crossly.

Marcus had straightened. "What did she say?"

"He's not answering his phone," Jenna relayed. To Katie she said, "He's probably gone to the office."

"Or he's sleeping off the hangover," Marcus suggested.

Katie said, "Maybe I should go and see if he's all right. I'll be late for work, but—"

"Hang on." Jenna put her hand over the receiver and caught at Marcus's sleeve as he made to leave. She and Katie both had bosses to placate if they were late; he didn't. He *was* the boss. "Could you go round by Dean's place," she pleaded, "and make sure he's okay?"

Marcus frowned. "He isn't a child. And he's not the type to top himself over a broken love affair."

"Katie's worried."

He took the phone from her. "Katie? I'll call in and see Dean before I go to the office, okay? Though it's my guess he'd rather be left alone.... Yes, I'll let you know if I think he needs you. Yes…promise."

Hanging up, he gave Jenna an exasperated look. "Personally I should think the last thing he wants is a lot of women fussing over him."

She was home earlier than Marcus that evening, making dinner as he arrived.

"I saw Dean," he told her. "He's sorry for himself and he had a hell of a head, but he went to work. He'll get over it."

Jenna had to remind herself that Marcus wasn't as callous as he sounded. He might be less openly emotional than the twins, but he was fond of them. When his family was in trouble he always came through for them.

She set the table in the dining area in the living room and turned on the light. As she was returning to the kitchen, a glint of something bright made her bend down, finding a tiny sliver of glass. Picking it up cautiously, she noticed that the door was scratched, a new scar on the lower part of it marring the varnish. For a second or two she studied it, puzzled.

She recalled that Marcus had dropped a glass last night—so he'd said.

But if he'd dropped it on the carpet in the living room, it wouldn't have broken. And if he'd been in the kitchen she would hardly have heard it so clearly from the bedroom.

Surely he couldn't have *thrown* it at the door? That would have been most unlike him. And why would he do such a thing?

A hissing noise and a pungent smell from the stove reminded her she'd left a pot of vegetables on high. She rushed to save it, and by the time she'd disposed of the glass, rescued the vegetables and cleaned up the mess they'd made, Marcus had emerged from the bedroom.

Halfway through the meal she remembered. "Where did you drop that glass?"

"What glass?"

"You said you dropped a glass last night."

"Is it important?" He picked up the one in front of him and took a sip before putting it down again. "I'm sorry if it was a special one."

"No, but…"

"You can always buy more," he said.

"Yes, I know." He set no limit on her spending, although she still used her own money to buy her clothes and cosmetics. "It's not that. I just wondered how you broke it. There's a mark on the door."

Marcus frowned. "Is there? Where?"

She pointed. "It's not very obvious, but..."

"Never mind," he interrupted. "We can get it fixed."

That wasn't the point, but he said, "Have you heard from your mother lately? She promised to send a newspaper article she thought would interest me."

Not wanting to nag, or make a mountain out of what was surely not more than a molehill, Jenna let the subject of the broken glass die.

Three days later a handyman fixed the door and it looked as good as new.

Over the following weeks Katie and Jenna did their best to make sure Dean didn't have too much time to brood. Not the kind to slink off and lick his wounds in private, he accepted invitations and hid his feelings behind a show of his usual effervescence.

Jenna asked him round for dinner, along with Katie and a few other friends. She and Katie asked him to take them to a craft show out of town that Marcus didn't want to attend, and Katie persuaded him to drive her to their parents' place for a Sunday lunch. When Marcus had a boat again for a weekend, Jenna suggested that they invite Dean along. Shrugging, Marcus agreed. "If you think it's a good idea."

"He needs to be kept occupied," she answered. "And he likes sailing. We can tell him we need an extra pair of hands."

Maybe he knew they didn't, but Dean came along anyway, and she thought he enjoyed himself. She took careful note so that she could report back to his sister, who she knew would call the next day to ask how he had seemed.

"It will take time," Jenna warned her. "We can't expect too much too soon."

"There's a pop concert in the Domain next Saturday," Katie said. "We'll take him to that."

They did, although Marcus refused to accompany them. "Not my favorite group," he said. "I didn't think it was yours, either."

It wasn't, but Katie seemed to take it for granted that she would go, as she assumed that if she wasn't available to entertain and distract Dean, Jenna would be.

Sometimes Jenna noticed the droop of his shoulders, or caught him in an unguarded moment, his mouth turned down and his eyes distracted, and a little reflection of his hurt tugged at her heart. Then he'd look up and smile at her, and she'd smile back, not letting on that she knew his casual, laid-back air hid very real pain.

Katie knew it too. She worried that Dean had lost weight, that he wasn't eating properly. She wondered aloud if she should get in touch with Callie and tell her how much Dean missed her, that he still loved her.

"For God's sake," Marcus said irritably, strolling into the living room one day as Jenna was lending a sympathetic ear to his sister, "let the guy sort himself out in his own way. He won't thank you for trying to solve his problems."

"We just want to help him," Katie said. "Don't you?"

"I don't see there's much we can do. If he really wants Callie—"

"Of course he wants her!" Katie was shocked. "He loves her!"

"Then why isn't he on a plane to the States?" Marcus asked bluntly.

"It's not that simple. He's got a job here to hold down," Katie protested. "He can't work in the States without a permit and Callie—"

"It seems to me that two people who really love each other should be able to work out some kind of compromise."

"Like what?" Katie challenged.

"Like making a commitment to Callie spending time with her family a couple of times a year. Like marrying her and then looking for work in the States. Like putting himself out to make her so happy with him she won't miss her own people as much."

Katie sniffed. "It's easy for you to say. You have plenty of money."

"Dean knows he only has to ask and he can have a loan anytime. And I didn't say it would be easy. Loving someone was never meant to be easy. Real love demands sacrifice and pain and damned hard decisions. It's gut-wrenching and soul destroying, and there are times when it seems more than a man can take. But you'll do anything, put up with anything just to be near the person you love, even if it hurts like hell. And you'll even give *that* up if necessary to give her her heart's desire."

Jenna stared at him, and Katie was openmouthed too.

Marcus clamped his lips into a line, and color appeared on his cheekbones. "If he doesn't love her that way," he said, "then he doesn't deserve her."

After he'd left the room, Katie looked at Jenna and lifted her brows interrogatively.

Jenna shook her head, as bewildered as his sister, and perturbed. She had never heard Marcus speak with such passion. Who was the woman who had inspired it? Her hands unconsciously curled in her lap. Her back went rigid. A fierce flame of jealousy ignited inside her.

Marcus had never pretended he felt anything that strong about her. She couldn't reproach him for deceiving her, because he hadn't.

Chapter Ten

Jenna broached the subject obliquely with Katie. "I know Marcus had girlfriends before me," she said, as they washed up after the family had come to dinner one night. "Was he serious about any of them?"

"Hard to say," Katie answered thoughtfully. "He didn't bring them home often, and you know Marcus—he's always played his cards close to his chest, especially about his personal life. Still," she added cheerfully, "I'm sure you've nothing to worry about. I shouldn't think any of them are likely to crawl out of the woodwork now, and if they did, he wouldn't look at them. He's much too...well, honorable, and apart from that, he loves you."

"I know," Jenna hastened to agree, taking the latter part of her friend's assurance with her customary grain of salt.

"Is there a problem?" Katie asked.

"No." Jenna shook her head. "Except one of his

friends said...she thought someone had hurt him.''
She remembered his assurance when they were in his
father's orchid house that the pain would pass, she'd
get over it. Had it passed for him? Had he really got
over his mystery lover?

Katie said, "Everyone's been hurt at some time. I
shouldn't think my big brother is the type to let any
woman blight his life...although," she added
thoughtfully, "still waters run deep and all that.
Maybe he just wouldn't admit it. You probably understand him better than any of us."

"Because I'm his wife?"

"Well, that, of course," Katie agreed. "But you
and Marcus are alike in so many ways. I guess that's
why you fell for each other."

Jenna blinked.

"Sort of enclosed and intense. Not like Dean and
me. We're all on the surface. Everyone knows when
we're happy. And when we want to hide something,
we just apply another glossy coat that looks like the
same thing to most people. I mean, look at him now."

Jenna nodded. She and Katie knew Dean was covering up, and sometimes he let the cheerful mask slip
with them, but outsiders would be fooled by his de-
terminedly cheerful, outgoing manner. They would
think his broken engagement was a minor glitch in a
carefree life.

Katie said, "I can tell with Dean. But I never know
what Marcus is thinking, even though he's my
brother. And you're more like him than I ever realized.... I thought that we knew all about each other,
though you don't blab about everything to me the way

I do to you. I know you have more secrets than I do. But I never suspected you had a thing for Marcus.''

"Maybe," Jenna said, thanking her stars that she'd never felt it necessary to tell Katie she'd been in love with Dean, "I didn't know it myself. I was so accustomed to thinking of Marcus as a surrogate big brother.''

Katie nodded wisely. "I guess that's why. And he was waiting for you to grow up.''

"That's what he said," Jenna admitted dryly. "Several times.'' Sometimes she wondered if even now he regarded her as truly grown-up.

It was true that Marcus seldom showed his feelings openly. She was pretty sure that if she asked him point-blank who the woman was, he would deny there had ever been any such person. It was all in the past anyway, and although she was his wife, it didn't seem she had any right to probe into his previous love life.

She couldn't help noticing that he seemed to be preoccupied these days. Sometimes she found him staring at her frowningly, seeming deep in thought, but if she queried him he'd say, "Sorry, I was thinking about something else.''

Maybe, Jenna deduced, he was as worried about Dean as she and Katie, although he seldom mentioned the subject. One Sunday she came upon him standing idly at the sitting room window, hands in his pockets and his shoulders uncharacteristically hunched.

"Marcus?" She crossed the room and hooked her hand into his arm. "Are you thinking about Dean?"

In profile his face looked hard and shuttered. It was a moment before he turned to her, pulling free. His eyes seemed oddly unseeing. "You could say so. Although you and Katie do enough of that for all of us."

"You're in a bad mood," she said. "Do you have business worries?" He never talked much about his business, but lately he'd spent a lot more time at the office than previously.

"Business is booming," he answered. Catching her hand in his, he looked down at it, then bent his head and dropped a kiss on the back. "I'm just a moody critter." He gave her a slightly twisted smile. But his eyes didn't match it.

"No, you're not," Jenna argued, then hesitated. "You would tell me if something was wrong, wouldn't you?"

He didn't answer at once. "That would depend on what it was. If there was nothing you could do about it, then very likely not."

"But we're married!" Didn't that mean they should share their troubles? Support each other in adversity?

"Yes," he agreed in a strange tone. "We're married. We've burned our boats, haven't we?"

"For better or worse," she agreed. His phrasing had seemed a little odd, though. She studied him seriously. "I really did mean that, Marcus." And she knew *he* had. Marcus would never go back on his solemn vows. "You're not sorry, are you?" she asked anxiously. He had seemed so sure, overriding her misgivings.

"How could I be sorry? Are you?"

Jenna vehemently shook her head. "Of course not. You're a wonderful husband." She reached up to give him a light kiss, but as her lips touched his he hauled her closer into his arms and kissed her properly, leaving her breathless.

When their mouths parted, he said, "Let's go to bed."

After the barest hesitation Jenna said, "I can't. I'm sorry, I promised Katie. We're going over to Dean's this afternoon. I came to ask if I could have the car. You did say you had paperwork to do."

"So I did." He swung both her hands in his. "I could do it tonight." His brows rose interrogatively.

Regretfully Jenna shook her head. "If I don't go, Katie will have to get a bus, and you know how they are on Sundays."

"Damn my family!" he said quite forcefully. "I think you spend more time with them than you do with me."

Not true, and it wasn't like him to exaggerate. "I owe them a lot."

"You don't owe any of us anything!" Marcus told her. "Except possibly my mother."

"Well…anyway, I promised," Jenna reiterated.

He looked at her rather keenly. "You never go back on a promise, do you, Jenna?"

"Not if I can help it. Neither do you."

He still held her hands. She felt his grip tighten slightly. "You didn't marry me because you felt you owed the family, did you?"

Astonished, Jenna said, "No!" Clumsily, because his probing eyes made her feel self-conscious, she added, "I married you because you asked me and…and I wanted to. And you were right—I…I do love you, Marcus."

He dropped her hands and cupped her face with his. "Thank you." His lips brushed against hers and lingered for a moment. "I'm counting on that."

When she came home later, he was deep in papers and using his laptop computer. He looked up rather remotely when she stopped to say hello, then his eyes focused on her and he said, "You look tired. What have you been doing?"

"Cleaning," she said. "It's amazing how quickly a place can get quite filthy. Katie told Dean he's living in a pigsty. It was only a slight exaggeration."

Marcus frowned. "Why doesn't he do his own cleaning?"

"I think he's too depressed to see the point of it. He did help once we got going."

"You two spoil him."

"He's going through a bad time."

"We all go through bad times. He'll work it out if he's left alone."

"That might be your way of coping," she pointed out, "but it isn't Dean's."

"Maybe," Marcus conceded. "You think I'm a heartless sod, don't you?"

"I know you're not. But you're stronger than Dean. I don't think you understand him the way..."

"The way you do?" Marcus supplied. Then he gave a short, harsh laugh. "You don't seem to have understood him as well as you thought, in the past."

Jenna flushed painfully, disconcerted at the oblique reference. It wasn't like Marcus to be callous. "I was going to say," she continued with dignity, "the way Katie does."

"Really?" He was regarding her with something

akin to disbelief. "And does Katie think he needs you as well as her to hold his hand?"

"Well, you seem to have been too busy to do it!" Jenna flashed, not that she could imagine Marcus holding his brother's hand exactly, but in the last few weeks he'd certainly been unavailable to his family on a number of occasions, pleading pressure of work. "You could at least show you care!"

To her surprise he looked uncomfortable for a moment, before he came back with, "Dean knows I care. Surely he doesn't need my shoulder to cry on too."

"What have you been so busy with lately, anyway? I've hardly seen you myself."

Marcus asked, "Do you miss me? Most of the time you're either with Dean or discussing his troubles with Katie."

Jenna gulped. Maybe it seemed that way to him. "That isn't true," she defended herself. "If you were home more you'd know."

He gazed at her. "Point taken," he said slowly. "I'm sorry if you've been feeling neglected."

"I didn't say that! I know you have a business to run."

"I also have a marriage to protect." He seemed to be looking at her rather carefully. "Burying my head in the sand—or work—isn't going to do any good, is it?"

Not sure what he meant, Jenna said, "Our marriage isn't in any danger, Marcus. Just because I've been spending time with Dean..." Surely he wasn't jealous? "I mean, that's not an issue."

"I'm glad to hear it." For a moment he seemed to be contemplating her, his eyes dark and strangely cool, almost analytical. Then he said abruptly, "You'd better go to bed. It'll be a while before I'm finished up here."

She went to bed and lay awake for a while, but soon tiredness overcame her. When Marcus came to join her she didn't wake, and when she woke in the morning the only evidence that he had shared their bed that night was the flung-back blankets and the indentation of his head on the pillow beside her.

He did spend more time at home after that night, yet paradoxically it seemed to Jenna that she and Marcus were growing further and further apart.

There was nothing she could put her finger on, no moment when things began to go wrong, no specific happening she could have cited. Sex was as sizzling as ever but it happened less often, and at other times Marcus appeared increasingly distant and almost abstracted.

Jenna told herself it was just that the honeymoon period of their marriage was over, but she sometimes thought wistfully that it had been awfully short.

She tried not to hope too much about the chances of having a baby, and when the calendar showed she was overdue she said nothing to Marcus. Better to wait until she could be sure.

Katie guessed first. She and Jenna were at her parents' house, putting the finishing touches to a family dinner celebrating Mrs. Crossan's birthday, when Jenna laid down the forcing bag she was using to pipe cream around a trifle and excused herself to rush to the bathroom.

When she came back Katie looked up from slicing

strawberries to add to the trifle, and said, "You're pregnant, aren't you?"

Jenna explained, "It's too early yet to be definite, and I haven't even said anything to Marcus. Don't tell anyone, will you?"

"I won't say a word," Katie promised. "You don't think Marcus suspects? It must be difficult keeping it a secret from him."

"I'm trying to for now." If she really was pregnant she wanted to surprise him, hoping the news would bring them closer again. She felt a faint shadow cross her face and banished it with an effort.

"He's bound to find out sooner or later."

"I'll tell him, of course, at the right time."

Thinking she heard a step in the hallway outside the kitchen, she turned her head, but there was no one there.

When it was time to drive home, Marcus handed Jenna the keys. "I've had a few glasses of wine," he said.

She had noticed him drinking more tonight than usual and had supposed that, as he was with his family and knew she wouldn't be overindulging, he'd thought it was safe to do so.

He leaned back in his seat and closed his eyes, and she wondered if he'd gone to sleep, but when she turned into their garage he was awake and alert, climbing out to open her door for her.

She brushed against him as she got out, the car key in her hand, and went toward the elevator.

When Marcus unlocked the door to their apartment the passageway inside was dark, and she groped for the light switch, encountering his hand doing the same.

His fingers curled around hers, and the light remained off. In the darkness he said her name and pulled her toward him. The car key dropped to the floor.

Startled, she put a hand to his chest, her palm against the body-warmed cotton of his shirt. She could smell his male scent, fresh and with an earthy hint of musk, and automatically she raised her face. Dimly she could just see his, a blacker outline against the blackness of the night.

Marcus found her mouth in a kiss that surprised her by its instant, primitive passion. With no preliminary at all he was kissing her deeply, thoroughly, almost aggressively.

She'd thought the unusual amount of wine had made him lethargic, but there was nothing lethargic about this. For several seconds she remained passive, trying to readjust to his mood after she had fully expected he would fall into bed and go straight to sleep.

His arms went about her waist, so tightly she could hardly breathe, her body a taut curving bow. She had to clutch his shoulders to keep her balance, then wound her arms about his neck.

She was tired, but her body was waking to the needs of his, her heart beginning a slow pounding while an answering passion stirred, sending a hot tremor through her.

He crowded her against the wall, and his hands shaped her breasts in an almost rough caress that brought them tinglingly to life. His hands tugged at the front of her dress and she was afraid he would tear it, but his mouth stifled her protest. Then he found the zip at the back and opened it with one decisive movement, hauled it off her shoulders and undid her bra.

Grabbing both garments, he finally released her mouth as he pulled them away from her.

"Marcus!" she gasped. "Be careful—"

He hoisted her into his arms and carried her the few steps to the bedroom, kicking the door shut before he lowered her to the bed.

She heard him strip off his clothes, and was still getting her breath when he lay beside her and quickly took off the rest of hers. "Marcus?" she said, nervous in the face of this silent, ruthless seduction.

"Shut up," he said, shocking her.

Suddenly she was afraid. Ridiculous, she assured herself. Drink had blunted his usual finesse, but Marcus would never hurt her, he would never force her. She trusted him utterly.

Nevertheless she was rigid when he took her in his arms. And he must have noticed. Although more than ready, he checked himself, held her while he took several deep breaths, and his touch gentled.

He didn't speak again, but his mouth brushed her temple, her cheek, the hollow of her throat, between her breasts, in soft, butterfly kisses. His hands shaped the contours of her body, lightly and knowingly, skimming over rib cage and hip and thigh, and his fingers teased the most sensitive erogenous spots.

Disturbingly, frustratingly, he kissed her everywhere except her mouth, until she felt as if a lambent fire was licking over her entire body, and she couldn't help begging at last, almost sobbing the words, "Marcus—please kiss me!"

He obliged with a soul-shattering, mind-obliterating kiss that was perfect in its blend of tenderness and passion, and she responded with her heart and soul. They were still kissing when he turned on his back and guided her onto his throbbing hardness.

She closed about him with a sigh of relief, moving ecstatically with him, until all too soon the marvelous release of tension took her over, and she was still whimpering with pleasure when Marcus turned again, thrusting deeply into her, bringing her to another pinnacle of passion, that became more intense when she knew he was there too. And just when she thought it was over she had to clutch at his shoulders again, heard his triumphant little laugh, and he watched her bite her lip as he helped her yet again over the brink.

She loved him. In every way, she loved him. The revelation blinded her.

Minutes later she opened her eyes to find him leaning on one elbow, still watching her. A high moon let white light into the room, but all she could see of his face was the sheen of his eyes.

"Marcus…"

He put his fingers over her mouth. "Don't talk. Not tonight."

Jenna didn't argue. She felt pleasantly exhausted—sated. She'd almost been going to mention the possible baby, but if she was wrong, she didn't want to disappoint him as well as herself.

In the morning she woke to find him watching her again, his expression brooding.

"You haven't been there like that all night, have you?" she asked him.

"No. Are you all right?"

"Of course."

"I'm sorry if I was a bit...insensitive last night."

"You weren't." She looked at him curiously. "You don't usually drink that much."

His eyes were suddenly bleak. "No I don't. And I won't again."

"I'm not complaining, Marcus," she said carefully. If anything, the episode had reassured her that no matter how importunate his own feelings, he would always take time and trouble to ensure that she enjoyed lovemaking too. He was never selfish.

"No," he said, and she was puzzled at the harshness of his voice. "You never complain, do you? A perfect wife."

Her brow knitted. "I'm not perfect... What have I done to annoy you?"

"What makes you think that?" he countered. "I just paid you a compliment."

Had he? It had sounded strangely like an accusation. But before she could challenge him on it, Marcus was out of the bed and shutting himself in the bathroom.

She must have imagined the rasping note in his voice, or perhaps the residue of sleep had produced it. Over the next few days he was, if anything, more loving—if that was the word for his slightly detached consideration and concern, and the watchfulness that sometimes unsettled her. She wondered if he had a suspicion she was pregnant.

Studying her while she cautiously nibbled on a

piece of toast one morning, he said abruptly, "Are you losing weight?"

"No!" She had no idea if she was, but the suggestion startled her. Today she'd woken feeling queasy, but most of the time she was fine. She hadn't had to dash to a bathroom after that one time at the Crossans'. Since then she'd kept away from rich foods and averted her eyes when she passed a bakery.

Hastily she took a bite of her toast and swallowed it.

"You should have a decent breakfast," Marcus said. "Toast and juice is hardly a meal." He had two poached eggs on his plate. "Have one of my eggs."

"No!" Jenna said. "I'm not used to a big breakfast. It would only make me feel...bloated." Actually she was sure it would make her feel sick. She could feel herself going pale already.

He made a little huffing sound of derision and looked over what he could see of her figure across the breakfast table. She saw a frown appear between his dark brows, and suddenly his eyes met hers.

"Do you have any plans for the weekend?" she asked quickly.

"I meant to tell you, Ted and Angela invited us to join them on their yacht. They're leaving on Friday night."

"Oh...um..." Sailing on possibly choppy waters didn't appeal right now. Her stomach churned just thinking about it. She had made a doctor's appointment for Friday after work. "The whole weekend?" she queried.

"Is it a problem?"

Jenna swallowed down disappointment. Supposing

the doctor confirmed the test she'd already secretly carried out, another couple of days before telling Marcus would make no difference. He loved sailing—he had plans to have a boat built of their own. "Why don't you go anyway? Katie wants me to go to the women's book fair over the weekend. I sort of promised." Not quite true, but she had told Katie it looked interesting.

"You didn't mention it."

"You didn't mention the Travers' invitation, either. I'll phone Angela and explain. We don't have to do everything together, do we?"

He pushed away his empty plate and stood up. "Are you feeling smothered, Jenna?"

"What makes you say that?"

"Except for a Friday-night get-together with your workmates, you spend most of your time with either me or my family. Do we give you enough space?"

"I have all the space I need." She wondered if *he* did. Marcus was accustomed to being alone a lot, or at least not having a wife to make emotional demands on him. Maybe that was the reason he was determined to preserve a sort of distance between them. She'd been married to him for six months and yet she sometimes felt she didn't know him any better than she had before their wedding.

Sunday she would tell him about the baby. When he was relaxed after a weekend sailing and they were alone for the evening, without any distractions or other commitments. If she was right.

She was, the doctor confirmed when she saw him on Friday, and the news made her feel giddy. Afraid to trust her own suspicion, or even the over-the-counter test despite its claims of accuracy, she had been holding in her emotions. Now she was dying to tell the world—but especially Marcus.

In the bathroom at home the atmosphere was slightly steamy, and a sleeve of Marcus's business shirt hung from the laundry basket, but he'd gone. She knew he'd planned on leaving the office early, and he must have taken a quick shower and changed before Ted and Angela picked him up to go to the marina. He'd left the car with her for the weekend so she and Katie could drive to the fair.

Stupid to be so disappointed. She'd had no intention of blurting out her secret right now. It would have been totally the wrong time. And Sunday was only forty-eight hours away.

At the book fair Jenna found her attention frequently wandering. While her face gave every appearance of absorption in the excellent presentations, her mind persisted in drawing pictures of a child with Marcus's dark hair and intent gray eyes—a solemn little boy or a winsome girl.

Katie had to nudge her when the panel discussion they'd attended was over. "Lunch," she said. "What do you fancy?"

"Nothing. Maybe a bread roll."

Katie eyed her suspiciously. "Have you seen a doctor yet?"

Jenna tried not to look smug. "I can't say anything until I've talked to Marcus."

Katie gave a squeak of excitement. "Haven't you *told* him?"

"I only found out for sure yesterday, and he's away for the weekend."

Katie hugged her. "Aren't you excited?"

Jenna allowed herself a smile. "I'm trying not to show it." She was saving it for the moment she told Marcus.

"I'm going to be an auntie to my best friend's baby!" Katie hugged her again. "Oh, this is great!"

She fussed over Jenna for the rest of the day, making sure she ate food that wouldn't upset a delicate-feeling stomach, and insisting that they arrive early for every event so that Jenna was assured of a comfortable seat.

On Sunday morning when Jenna got into the car and turned the key, nothing happened. After a few frustrating minutes she realized that the interior light was burning, although she didn't recall switching it on. The battery must have drained overnight.

Katie was waiting to be picked up. Jenna returned inside and phoned her.

"Dean's here," Katie informed her. "He can take us. We'll collect you on the way."

On their arrival at the venue, Dean looked interestedly at one of the posters outside. "I read that book," he said, indicating the cover of an account of a woman climber's expedition in the Himalayas.

"She's speaking this morning," Katie informed him. "Why don't you buy a ticket and come in?"

"With all those women?"

It took a bit more persuasion, but eventually he said, "Well, I don't have anything better to do, I guess."

As he was buying a ticket, Jenna said sadly to his sister, "He's still hurting, isn't he?"

Katie agreed. "Callie phoned him last week."

"She did? Why?"

Katie shrugged. "Just to see how he was, she said."

"She still cares."

"I guess. But if she's not coming back it might be better if she didn't get his hopes up."

Surprisingly, Dean stayed for the day and after a talk by a psychologist about male-female relationships, he even bought a copy of her book.

Afterward he dropped off his sister first. When they arrived at Jenna's apartment he took a jumper lead from his car and started the dead battery, accepting Jenna's offer of coffee when he'd finished. She had the feeling he didn't want to go home. He'd spent the previous night at Katie's after dropping in for a nightcap.

They chatted for a while, and watched the first part of the TV news before Dean got up to go. He looked at her keenly, his head cocked. "Are you expecting?"

"Did Katie give me away?"

"She was just sort of watching you and waiting on you. That's not like her."

"I still have to tell Marcus."

Dean grinned. "He'll be chuffed." The grin faded and became a little twisted. "I'm jealous."

"Oh, Dean!" She put her arms about him in a comforting hug. "Things will work out."

He hugged her back, burying his face against her hair. "She phoned me—Callie," he said in muffled tones.

"I know," Jenna said. "Have you thought about going to see her?"

Dean lifted his head. "I think about nothing else. It's tearing me in two. I want to get on a plane tomorrow—tonight—and grab her and make her marry me. I think she'd do it too. But in another three months, or six months or a year, maybe she'd find she couldn't hack it after all."

Jenna supposed that was a point. "You're sure you couldn't find a job over there?"

"Not legally, unless we're married."

"So…couldn't you do that?"

He frowned distractedly. "The trouble is, it feels like blackmail to persuade her to marry me so I can work in America."

"Even though it's because you love her and want to be with her?"

"See, I already put the heat on to persuade her to come home with me, but she wouldn't commit herself to marriage. Being engaged was a sort of compromise. I can't pressure her again." His voice shook. "But I love her so much."

The misery in his face wrung her heart, and she put one hand to his cheek. "I hate to see you hurting like this."

"Some mistakes you just have to live with, because trying to fix them will only make things worse."

"Could it be worse?" Jenna asked as his hold on her loosened. "Two people who love each other so much should be together! There must be a way…"

"It isn't that easy. How would *you* feel," Dean said, "if I asked you to choose between your family and the man you love?"

Jenna hadn't had the kind of family that Callie did, but she'd wanted one so badly it didn't take much imagination. She said, "I think I'd feel as though I'd lost a leg and an arm." But if the unthinkable happened, of course she would choose Marcus. There was no doubt in her mind.

A movement caught from the corner of her eye made her turn her head, and she was startled to see Marcus standing in the doorway.

Dean was taken by surprise too. He dropped his arms and ran a hand over his hair as though embarrassed. Jenna thought that surreptitiously he was also wiping at a wayward tear.

Understanding that he didn't want his brother to see him crying, she took a step toward Marcus in an instinctive shielding movement and put a smile on her mouth. "We didn't hear you come in," she said. The TV still murmuring in the background must have covered the sound of his entry. "I didn't expect you so early."

"Apparently not." He looked grim and cold.

"Hi, Marc," Dean said with false brightness just behind her. "How was the fishing?"

Marcus flicked him a glance. "What are you doing here?"

Quelling a stupidly alarmed flutter in her throat, Jenna explained, "Dean drove me home. The car was dead this morning—a flat battery."

"There was nothing wrong with the battery when I drove it on Friday."

"Somehow I left the interior light on. It's all right now. Dean fixed it and I invited him for coffee."

Silly. She had never found it necessary to give

Marcus chapter and verse when she invited anyone in, and Dean was family, for heaven's sake!

"I was just on my way." Dean sounded as nervous as she felt. He made toward the door that Marcus was still blocking, and hesitated in front of his brother.

Marcus seemed to be inspecting him. Then he stood aside, his attention concentrated on Jenna.

"Well…" Dean looked around rather helplessly. "See you. Thanks for the coffee, Jenna."

"Thank you," she said, "for the car and everything." One of them should see him out, but something kept her rooted where she stood, and Marcus certainly wasn't moving.

There was a tense silence as the outer door closed behind Dean.

"How long has he been here?" Marcus asked.

She blinked at him. "I don't know…about half an hour, I think, since fixing the car."

"Not the whole weekend?"

Her eyes widened in astonishment. "No. He came to the book fair today with Katie and me. Last night he was at her flat."

"And where were you last night?"

"Here, of course!" Incredulously she said, "Marcus—you're sounding like a suspicious husband!"

The idea was so ludicrous she couldn't help a small laugh.

"So I am," he said, and she thought he made a conscious effort to relax, his hands going into his pockets, although his eyes stayed watchful. "Are you telling me I don't have reason to be?"

Jenna gaped. "I told you, Dean gave Katie and me

a lift because the car wouldn't start. He came to the fair with us.''

"Doesn't sound like Dean's sort of thing," Marcus commented skeptically.

"Ask Katie if you don't believe me."

He was looking at her thoughtfully. Softly he said, "Katie would back up her twin in anything he said. You too. The three of you always stuck together."

"We're not kids now!"

"No," Marcus said, still in that soft tone of deadly mockery. "That's exactly my point."

Chapter Eleven

Jenna's head buzzed. "I don't believe this!" she gasped. The quarrel had blown up so unexpectedly, wrecking her plans for a quiet, loving evening, the revelation of a happy secret. "You're jealous!"

"Damn right I am," Marcus agreed calmly, the chill in his eyes, the rigid planes of his face, belying his tone.

"You've always been jealous!" she realized. This was about more than finding her exchanging an innocent hug with his brother.

It went right back to their childhood, when she and the twins had been nearly inseparable and Marcus, the big brother, was almost one of "them"—the adults. Outside the tight little circle of three.

Surprisingly, a line of color darkened his cheekbones. His jaw jutted. "I have a right now," he said.

A right to what? "To accuse me? Just what *are* you accusing me of, Marcus?" She glared at him, her own cheeks hot, her eyes ablaze.

He looked back at her, and she met his gaze unflinchingly. "What do you think I've done?" she challenged him. "Spent the weekend in bed with Dean? *Our* bed?" She took a shaky breath. "Do you really believe that?"

The hint of color disappeared from his face, leaving it drained and white. "No," he said, as if the word was forced out between stiff lips. One hand rubbed at his forehead, and he closed his eyes. For an instant she thought he swayed where he stood. "No," he repeated, dropping his hand.

There was a bleak weariness in his eyes. "I apologize, Jenna. Excuse me—I need a shower, and all my clothes smell of fish. I've put some snapper fillets in the fridge. Ted's taken a couple of kahawai home to smoke for us."

The sudden descent to banality did nothing to dissipate the tension in the air. He had left the room before Jenna got her breath back, and shortly afterward she heard the shower running. It ran for a long time, and then the washing machine began its swishing cycle.

Meantime, on legs that felt rubbery, she got herself into the kitchen. Looking at the fillets that Marcus had brought home, she wondered if she should change the menu and cook them but decided they would keep for tomorrow. Listlessly she put the finishing touches to the celebration dinner she'd planned.

She'd made the chicken and cashew salad yesterday. It would taste better after a day of being permeated by its special dressing, needing only a garnish of asparagus tips and toasted almond slices. Mechanically she shredded lettuce, sliced tomatoes and avocado and drizzled them with vinaigrette.

The candles in their crystal holders no longer seemed appropriate, so she left them on the kitchen counter, took the bottle of champagne from the fridge and hid it in the pantry. She'd thought she might be having a token sip or two in celebration, but the bruising encounter just now had killed her mood of joyous anticipation, leaving her sick and scared.

Instead she put a half-used bottle of still white wine by Marcus's place and set a glass there before pouring some mineral water for herself.

She was putting the salad on the table when Marcus came in, his hair damp and his lean cheeks freshly shaved. He wore a white shirt, open at the throat, and dark trousers. His eyes met hers only fleetingly, seemingly without expression, and then he went to the table. "It looks good."

An olive branch, perhaps.

Jenna pushed her hair back over one ear as she took her chair. A shower and a change into something soft and pretty had been on her original agenda, but time had run out before Marcus arrived. The cotton shirt and jeans she was wearing would have to do. She'd probably lost the makeup she had put on earlier in the day, but it didn't seem to matter now.

She picked up the salad servers and transferred a few greens to her plate, followed by a spoonful of chicken.

Marcus helped himself, then glanced at her much smaller meal. "Surely you can eat more than that," he said.

Jenna didn't feel like eating anything at all. "I'll

have more if I want it.'' She dug her fork into the chicken and had to clench her teeth to make the food go down her throat and stay there. Trying to distract herself, she said, ''It's nice of Ted to smoke your fish for us.''

''He and Angela sent their love.''

Jenna nodded and made herself eat some more. ''The fishing must have been good. I could make a raw fish salad tomorrow,'' she said. ''Or would you prefer it cooked?''

''Whatever suits you.''

They were being stiffly polite, and Jenna could have wept. She finished what was on her plate and waited for him. ''Do you want any more?'' she asked.

He shoved his plate away, shaking his head, then said perfunctorily, ''It was delicious.''

She had the feeling that he hadn't tasted it any more than she had. ''There's passion fruit mousse. I'll get it.''

''I don't want any! Jenna—sit down.''

She sat, waiting for him to speak again. He had half a glass of wine in front of him, his hand restlessly twirling the stem. His gaze was fixed on the glass, and when he raised his eyes they were dark and steady. Almost gently, he said, ''Do you have something to tell me?''

He knew? Her breath caught, and she fought an urge to laugh hysterically. Everyone seemed able to guess without being told. Was it that obvious?

She tried to smile. This moment shouldn't be spoiled by a foolish spat. ''Yes, I do,'' she said, and watched his hand curl about the wineglass, so tightly she thought the fragile stem would surely snap. "I'm pregnant."

She thought the silence would never end; it was as though the whole world stood still. Then Marcus slowly, stiffly, uncurled his fingers. She thought he was going to reach out to her, but instead the hand tightened into a fist on the table, and he stared down at it. "Pregnant," he repeated, as if he'd never heard the word before. And then, "Oh, God!"

He shoved back his chair and got up, taking a few swift strides away from her, then turned to look at her again.

She didn't understand his reaction at all. "Aren't you pleased?"

He didn't look pleased. He looked as though he didn't know how he felt. Something flared in his eyes and died. "Are *you?*" he queried abruptly.

"I *was.*" But everything had gone wrong somehow. "I thought you wanted a family!"

"What I *want*—" he started in a furious undertone, and cut himself off there. When he spoke again his voice was perfectly even. "The point is, what do *you* want, Jenna? What do you really want most in all the world?"

A strange question to ask her now. She couldn't comprehend what had triggered it. "To have this baby," she said, "and give it a loving home, security, a happy childhood. Everything that parents want for their children."

"Everything you missed out on."

The comment caught her unawares. She had never thought of herself as neglected or missing out on a normal family life. Other children had solo mothers too. "It wasn't easy for my mother after my father died, and no one, until your mother, realized she was suffering from depression and could be helped with proper medical advice. But she loved me and did her best for me." Even though at times she had seemed faraway, scarcely noticing that she had a daughter at all. "And your family gave me a lot of leftover love."

"Leftover love?" he queried. "Is that what it felt like?"

She hesitated. "Spilled over, maybe. There was so much of it in your home. Your mother was always there for me, filling in the gaps. And the twins."

Marcus too had been there for her—he'd picked up the pieces of the heart she had broken over Dean, and made it whole.

Showing again that he could follow her thoughts, Marcus said, "And Dean?"

"That's over," she said. "You were right, I should have grown out of it much sooner than I did. I don't know what on earth you thought when you walked in tonight, but it wasn't…anything that need worry you." Gaining confidence, she told him, "You're my husband, the father of my child…" She paused then, but his expression didn't alter. "The man I intend to spend my life with, to the end of my life. I love you."

The acknowledgment set free something inside her, like a light bursting into life. She loved Marcus in every way—as a friend, a lover, the one person she wanted to be with forever. He was everything she'd ever dreamed of in a man, and more.

"Very noble," he said, the words like a slap in the face. "I'm touched."

Jenna winced, her temples throbbing. "Marcus—please!"

He said harshly, "This whole sorry mess is my fault. I should never have asked you to marry me."

That took her breath away, sent her heart plunging horribly.

She had just said she loved him, and he was rejecting her. Had she left her declaration too late? Or had he found that marriage to her wasn't enough to make him happy?

He had never said he was in love with her—not in the way that he'd been with that mysterious woman who had broken his heart. Their marriage had been founded on mutual liking and understanding and their lifelong knowledge of each other, combined with the sexual spark that had ignited into unexpected, white-hot flame.

Hurt and stirring resentment turned to panic and broke through her bewilderment. "What the hell do you mean by that?" she demanded, her voice rising. "I'm having your baby!"

"And that's my fault too," he said. "I should never have let you—"

"If you're having second thoughts, it's too late. I won't have an abortion, Marcus!"

His face paled again. "I wouldn't suggest it!"

"Then what are you suggesting? I thought this was what we both wanted."

He seemed to be considering that. "I was wrong," he said finally. "I told myself it would work, that I could make it work for both of us. I respect your integrity, Jenna, your determination to do the right thing. You keep telling me I have no need for jealousy, you intend to stick to your vows. But…I'm greedy.''

"Greedy?''

His smile was twisted. "I hustled you into marrying me even though I'd promised myself—and you—that I wouldn't. I should have known that leftover love is never enough.''

And that was all he could give her? "But then…'' she said, thinking aloud, "that was all you expected of *me,* wasn't it?''

It wasn't his fault that she had fallen into deep, irrevocable love that he was unable to return.

She got up and blindly collected the plates and cutlery, rattling them together as he said remotely, "True. It was all I asked for.''

Humiliation made her cheeks burn. "Well, I'm sorry,'' she said, turning to flounce out of the room before he saw the tears stinging her eyes. "I can't help it if you got more than you bargained for.''

Her vision blurred as she entered the kitchen, and when she made to put the plates on the counter she missed. With a crash and a clatter everything landed on the floor, a plate breaking in half, knives and forks scattering.

She dashed a hand across her eyes and was on her knees picking up the pieces when Marcus appeared in the doorway. "What happened?''

"What do you think?'' she countered viciously. "I dropped them.''

He bent and helped her, dumping the knives and forks and the undamaged plate into the sink. He even took the broken pieces of china from her and wrapped them in newspaper ready to be disposed of.

Not wanting to face him, Jenna turned to the sink and began washing up. There was a dishwasher but she tended to use it only when they were entertaining.

As she squirted detergent and began scrubbing at the remaining plate, she sensed Marcus standing just behind her. Her shoulders stiffened.

"I didn't mean to upset you," he said. "Your news caught me off guard, after…"

"I thought you already knew. Suspected, anyway. Everyone else did."

"Everyone?"

"Katie guessed, and I'm sure your mother knows although she didn't say anything. Even Dean…" She put the plate on the drying rack and fished in the water for the cutlery.

"Oh, yes. Dean. Is that what the big renunciation scene was all about?"

Jenna dropped the forks she held back into the water. She swung to face him. "What big renunciation scene?"

"You and Dean," Marcus said impatiently. "Deciding to live with your mistake."

It took a couple of seconds for the penny to drop. "Dean's mistake! Not mine."

"Has he finally realized what he missed, what he could have had if he hadn't been so blind all those years?"

"Were you drinking before you came home?" It was the only logical reason she could think of for his wild accusations and illogical conclusions.

"I'm stone-cold sober."

"Then what's the matter with you?" How could he have thought…?

He put a hand on either side of her, trapping her against the counter. "Nothing that hasn't been the matter ever since I married you—no, before that. Because I was stupid enough to fall in love with a girl who was so besotted with my brother she hardly even knew I existed. And even more stupidly, I deluded myself that marriage might bring about a miracle and make her love me back."

Jenna found she couldn't breathe, though her mouth had fallen open. "Me? You were in love with *me?*"

"From when I came back from overseas and found that the gawky kid I remembered had turned into a gorgeous young woman, and without losing any of the qualities I'd loved about her all my life." Witheringly he said, "You had no idea, did you?"

No, she hadn't. "B-but you never said…you never…you never did *anything!*"

Marcus scowled. "It was glaringly obvious that the only man you had eyes for was Dean. I did wonder sometimes if he felt the same way. It's hard to tell with Dean because he hides his deeper emotions, when he has them, under that party-boy manner of his. And it's not true that I never said anything."

She looked blank. "I don't remember anything that could have…"

"I dropped heavy hints, but you didn't want to hear them. Since it was plainly useless and would only embarrass you, I gave up. At one stage I had thought, The hell with it, I wanted you so much I would risk everything—your scorn, hurting Dean, causing a disruption in the family. And when he went overseas…"

Feeling her way, Jenna said, "So then, why didn't you—"

"That would have been dirty play, wouldn't it? Wait until he's out of the country and then make my move?"

Dimly she saw that he would have felt that. Anything sneaky or unfair would have been anathema to him.

"I was hamstrung," Marcus said. "I told myself there were other women who weren't fixated on their childhood sweethearts, women who wouldn't stir up a hornets' nest in the family, maybe split it apart. But I couldn't get you out of my mind, out of my heart."

"I had no idea!"

"I know that!" He looked at her somberly. "I've messed up your life, Jenna—yours and my brother's. And I'm truly sorry."

She clutched the front of his shirt. "Marcus—I love you!"

"Oh, sure. Much the same way you love my parents and Katie—with the added fillip of sex thrown in."

"No, you don't understand!" She tried to shake him, only succeeding in tearing a button off his shirt. It dropped and rolled on the floor. "Marcus—" The adolescent yearning she'd had for Dean was a trickling, shallow stream compared with the wide, deep ocean of her love for Marcus. "It's not the same, it's—"

"I don't need a sop, Jenna," he said roughly.

And then the phone rang.

"Leave it," she said, but her fingers released the fabric of his shirt as he turned away.

He lifted the receiver with a curt, "Yes?"

She saw him frown. "How much?" he asked. "Why?"

Listening intently, he looked over at her, his expression strange. There was a long pause, then he said, "Yes, I'm still here. Of course you can have it. I told you, anytime. I know I'll get it back, not that it matters. Come to the office tomorrow and I'll have it ready."

He put the receiver down and stood looking at it. "That was Dean," he said, raising his eyes. He looked stunned, puzzled. "Asking for a loan to fly to America."

"He's going to see Callie?"

"Apparently."

"Oh, good!"

"Is it?" He seemed dazed.

"Of course!" Jenna said impatiently. "Now do you believe me?" she beseeched him. "It isn't Dean I want, Marcus. It's you."

He passed a hand over his forehead. "Then what the hell were the two of you talking about when I came in?"

"Callie, of course!"

"*Callie?*"

"Dean didn't want to force her to choose between him and her family. But she phoned him this week, and I guess that gave him some hope. He loves her a lot."

"And you don't mind?"

How was she going to get through to him? "*I'm not in love with Dean!* I know I thought so, but that was just what you said—a childish daydream. *You* made me see that! Why won't you accept it?''

He said slowly, ''What were you and Katie talking about at my mother's birthday party?'' When she looked blank, he said, ''In the kitchen, before dinner.''

''Oh, then! She guessed I was pregnant. I made her promise not to tell because I wanted you to be the first to know. I had it confirmed on Friday but you'd arranged to go sailing and I didn't want it rushed so I thought…tonight, and I made a special dinner and chilled some champagne, but…'' She stopped there because her voice was trembling and she didn't want to burst into tears.

Marcus said, ''And after weeks of soul-searching, I had made up my mind that the only decent thing to do was tell you to go to Dean if he was the one you wanted, to set you free. Because it wasn't fair for me to hold you when he was no longer committed. Then you threw me a curve ball about the baby. And made that brave little speech about spending your life with me.''

''It wasn't brave!'' she objected. ''It was true.''

As if he hadn't heard, he continued, ''I wondered if you were trying to convince me or yourself. I'd just decided to set things right, and it was too late. A baby complicated matters even further. The implications were horrendous. And yet…I couldn't help being glad that you were carrying my child. Couldn't help wanting it, and wanting you. Even though you'd be trapped in a marriage you'd realized was a mistake.''

''Oh, Marcus! It wasn't a mistake! It was the best thing I ever did. What do I have to do to convince you *I love you!* Not as a brother—as a lover and a wonderful, sexy, incredibly giving husband.''

Hot tears spilled over and she gulped back a sob. The stress of the last couple of hours was telling, and the room began to sway.

Marcus made a low exclamation, swooping forward to catch her up in his arms.

''I don't want to be free!'' She wound her arms about his neck as he carried her into the bedroom. ''I want to be your wife and have your babies and love you forever!'' she told him passionately.

''Shh,'' he soothed, and deposited her on the wide bed, saying, ''Don't move.''

She let her arms fall and lay there, tears dripping silently onto the pillow, while he went into the bathroom and came back with a cool wet cloth that he laid on her brow. He wiped the tears away with a tissue and after a while they stopped. His hand turned the cloth over. ''Better?'' he asked quietly.

''Yes.'' She saw his face was drawn, his eyes worried. ''Sorry about that. Pregnancy does funny things to a woman.''

He shook his head. ''I can't tell you how sorry *I* am! Jealousy does funny things to a man,'' he said wryly. ''I've been fighting it for so long, in the end I couldn't keep the beast in its cage.''

''Oh, please don't! You have no need to feel that way,'' she said. She took his hand and pressed it to her lips. ''Marcus, darling Marcus—I love you in every way there is. And if you don't believe me this time, I think I'll die.''

His hand tightened on hers. ''If that's true,'' he said

hoarsely, "then I'm the happiest man on earth. And the luckiest."

Jenna smiled up at him. "You're the happiest man on earth," she said. "And I'm the luckiest woman."

"Jenna…"

She stretched her arms up to him, and he fell into her embrace. He said her name again and kissed her, hard and hungry and long.

"I love you," she whispered, a little later, parting the rest of the buttons on his shirt and pressing kisses down his chest.

He unzipped her jeans and eased them off, splaying a hand over her belly. "I don't see any sign of our baby."

"It's too early yet. My breasts are changing already, though."

"Let me see?" His hand went to her bra, and she lifted her shoulders to let him take it off. "You're blushing," he teased, raising his eyes from his inspection. He touched her with great care and her heartbeat increased its rhythm, a delicious warmth invading her body. "They're beautiful," he said, stroking the newly tender skin. "You are beautiful."

"You might not say that in a few months' time."

"I'll always say that," he told her firmly. "I can't wait to see you all round and womanly with my child. I'm so sorry—"

She put her hand over his mouth. "Just make love to me, please."

Her fingers were pressed to his heart, and he said, "I want to make love to you night and day for the next fifty years or more."

"You haven't been, lately."

He looked up from feathering kisses across her shoulders. "I was so eaten up with rage over Dean splitting up with Callie and you spending all that time consoling him—and so sure you couldn't help but regret marrying me when you might have had him after all. I didn't dare bring all that anger and bitterness into our bed, souring our lovemaking."

And she'd had no idea of his feelings, his suffering. How could she have been so blind? But Marcus had a great deal of practice at concealing his emotions. All these years he'd been hiding them from her…from everyone.

She touched his hair, wanting to comfort him for the hurts of the past and assure him of their future. "Katie and I…" she said, starting to explain.

"I know, Dean needed support, comfort." He lifted his head briefly. "You and Katie rallied round as always." He kissed her quickly on the mouth.

"That's all it was, Marcus." She willed him to accept the truth. "Supporting a friend. Oh…" she added breathlessly as his mouth moved lower. "That's…do it again."

"With pleasure," he purred, and obliged. She clutched at his hair.

"I'm not hurting you?" he asked.

"No!" she gasped, and heard his brief, deep laugh.

"If only you'd told me how you felt," she said, trying to breathe normally while his lips and hands sent thrills from her toes to her breasts. "Even when you proposed."

She had left it almost disastrously late to confess her love, but equally, he had given her no inkling of his real feelings.

Marcus lifted her knee and caressed her thigh. "I thought it might frighten you off marrying me," he said. "Knowing you, I had a hunch you'd feel you were cheating if you knew how much I loved you and that you would turn me down out of some misguided sense of fairness."

His touch made her catch her breath with delight. He smiled and dropped another kiss on her mouth. "Besides," he admitted, his voice slurring a little as his mouth explored other places, "knowing you couldn't feel the way I did, I was damned if I was going to surrender the last shred of my male independence."

"Ch-chauvinist," she accused him. She was trying to keep her mind off the increasingly exciting things he was doing with his fingers.

"Witch," Marcus said lovingly, and smiled into her eyes before he kissed her again.

Their lovemaking had always been sensational, but this time an extra element entered it. No holding back, no reservations, no secrets. They gave to each other and received in equal measure, together as they had never been before, in the most intimate way possible.

Afterward they lay in each other's arms in perfect contentment, whispering words that had been uttered by lovers since time immemorial, but for them were new and wonderful, like the evening star that peeked at them through the window as they talked about the coming baby, the miracle of their new knowledge and the years that stretched ahead of them.

Chapter Twelve

The Crossans' garden was filled with people enjoying champagne and snack food.

Bees hummed in the brilliant open blooms of the orange and red hibiscus and over the extravagant little pink blooms of the manuka. A white-and-orange-spotted black butterfly dipped and swirled as Jenna sat on the old wooden seat around the puriri, looking down at the baby she had just discreetly fed.

Her son stared back at her, his eyes wide and solemn. Already they were like his father's, the same fathomless dark gray.

"How's my godson?" Dean stood before her, a glass in his hand, his other arm about a radiant Callie.

"He's fine," Jenna answered. Her eyes went past them, looking for Marcus in the throng on the lawn.

As if he'd felt her gaze, he turned from speaking to two of the guests and strolled over to join them. His hand went to his brother's shoulder even as he smiled at Jenna and the baby. "Isn't that young man asleep yet?"

"He's too interested in what's going on," Jenna said.

Callie bent to offer a finger, and the newly christened Simon Marcus Crossan obligingly curled his tiny hand about it, cooing.

Enchanted, Callie looked up at her husband. "I want one of these."

Dean grinned at her. "I'm sure it could be arranged. We'd better decide if it's going to be an American or a Kiwi."

Callie wrinkled her nose. "I guess a Kiwi would be okay." She and Dean had been married in the States, but agreed that he shouldn't quit his New Zealand job in less than a year. After that, he had promised, if Callie was still pining for her home he'd try for work in America.

Katie joined the group, the hand hooked into Jason's arm sporting a brand-new engagement ring. "How's my godson?" She unconsciously parroted her twin.

Jenna laughed. Simon opened his mouth in a yawn, and then let out a fretful squawk. "Ready for bed," Jenna said, rising. "I'll just put him down."

"I'll come too." Marcus put his arm about her and accompanied her into the house.

Upstairs, she tucked the baby into the portable crib and soothed his sleepy protest with hushed words and a gentle hand, until his eyes closed.

Marcus looped his arms around her from behind, and they both gazed down at the small miracle they'd created. He said, "I never thought I could love you more than I did on our wedding night, but when you gave birth to our baby, I realized I'd been wrong. I never imagined one man could be so lucky.''

''You were wonderful that night,'' she told him.

''Which?'' He turned her in his arms, looking down at her quizzically.

She laughed up at him. ''Both. Both times you were strong when you needed to be, tender when it mattered. Caring. I love the way you've always cared for me. And I want to care for you too. You and our children.''

''Children...plural?'' he teased. ''Isn't one enough of a handful for now?''

''For now. But we have plenty of love left over for more, don't we?''

''Of course we do. We have so much we can't contain it all. More than enough for a family.''

She slid her arms about his neck. ''I love you!'' She knew she couldn't say it too often for him. She liked saying it, watching the light that kindled in his eyes every time.

''And I love you,'' he replied, but she hardly heard the words because they were uttered against her mouth, just before he kissed her, putting his heart and soul into a wordless pledge, a promise for the future, while their son slept peacefully beside them, secure in his parents' spilled-over love.

* * * * *

▼ Silhouette®

INTIMATE MOMENTS™
is proud to present

Romancing
the Crown

*With the help of their powerful allies,
the royal family of Montebello is determined
to find their missing heir. But the search for the
beloved prince is not without danger—or passion!*

**This exciting twelve-book series begins in January and
continues throughout the year with these fabulous titles:**

Available at your favorite retail outlet.

▼™ Silhouette®
Where love comes alive™

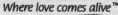